FAIRYTALE BUREAU
BOOK THREE

EVE LANGLAIS

Belle's Quest © 2024 Eve Langlais

Cover by Addictive Covers © 2024

Produced in Canada

Published by Eve Langlais

http://www.EveLanglais.com

E-ISBN: 978 177 384 5067

Print ISBN: 978 177 384 5074

ALL RIGHTS RESERVED

This book is a work of fiction and the characters, events and dialogue found within the story are of the author's imagination and are not to be construed as real. Any resemblance to actual events or persons, either living or deceased, is completely coincidental.

No part of this book may be reproduced or shared in any form or by any means, electronic or mechanical, including but not limited to digital copying, AI training, file sharing, audio recording, email and printing without permission in writing from the author.

Prologue

Agatha, AKA Fairy Godmother, left the ball hosted in honor of the Corsican prince quite pleased with how things had turned out. She'd managed to put another cursed Grimm story back in the book where it belonged. But it hadn't been easy.

It took much to counter the Grimm Effect's attempts to force Cinder and Prince Killian to marry. The curse kept trying to force the issue, even as it became quickly obvious Cinder had feelings for another. It hadn't been easy getting the reluctant Knight, Levi, to admit he loved Cinder, but now the pair were married and quite romantically too. When faced with possible death or marrying the prince, Cinder eschewed her safety and chose true love.

With Cinderella having foiled the Grimm Effect quite spectacularly, The Little Ash story returned to being just fiction. However, too many stories remained at large, with more being added. See, the Grimm Effect reenacted its own perverse version of the stories it had absorbed since its arrival from space.

Yes, space. A tiny little rock that Agatha had plucked from her garden, never realizing what she'd unleash.

Agatha glared at the side table in her study piled with books, a stack that had grown despite ridding her home of literature. The villagers kept popping by while she was forced to do her godmotherly duties. Although the true blame belonged to the alien stone at the heart of all their problems. It kept finding ways to add to its cursed magic. The latest addition? A compilation of Mother Goose's rhymes. Only the image on the cover remained to identify the tome that sat atop the pile, the pages in it blank, as the old lyrical poems were set loose on the world.

"Naughty stone. You've been busy while I was gone." She shook her finger at it but, of course, received no reply—

"You shouldn't be working against me."

The monotone voice startled. Agatha just about fell over, whipping around to see the strangest sight—which said a lot considering the things she'd observed since the stone's arrival.

A figure stood by the bookcase, not human, not

even alive. The papier-mâché simulacrum of a person crossed its arms as it stared at her—or so she assumed. Hard to tell since it lacked eyes.

"Who are you?" she exclaimed. "What are you doing in my home?"

"I am here because that is where my kernel of existence landed. I am known on your world as Methuselah."

"As in Methuselah from the bible? Or Methuselah the star?"

"Neither. Your astronomers have long miscategorized my existence," it corrected. "The only thing they got correct was my galactic origin."

"So not a star, but an alien." A chill went through her at the realization the tiny meteor she'd found in her garden was even more than she suspected. "But that makes no sense. Rocks aren't alive."

"There are many kinds of existence. The flesh-based version being the most basic."

"Basic and yet you made yourself a golem in our image," she pointed out.

"Because it seemed the most practical shape. And I am not a simple golem. Those are usually mindless puppets, whereas I am sentient. This"—it waved a hand at its body—"is merely a temporary container for my spirit."

"And why do you need a container?" Up until

now, this so-called Methuselah had been screwing over the world just fine without hands.

"That I might further my goals. It took longer than expected to gather the needed energy to create a vessel that could communicate. But I have plans to upgrade."

That sounded ominous. "I'm not sure I understand why you need a body. You've been meddling for decades without one." She couldn't help that sour observation.

"Because it is time for the next step in my conquest." The thing cocked its head, and she'd have sworn it sounded amused when it said, "Did you think I wouldn't notice you trying to thwart me?"

Rather than deny, she lifted her chin. "Can you blame me? You're ruining my planet."

"Ruining it how?"

"You're forcing people to act out perverted versions of fairytales." The Grimm stories could be dark enough without the alien rock twisting them into a curse.

"I don't see the problem."

"Do you even care you're ruining lives?" she blurted out.

"No."

"So what is your end goal?" Because she couldn't see it.

"To feed until I regain my former glory. I used to

be known as the devourer of worlds until I ran out of sentient planets. I spent an eternity starving, shrinking into almost nothing. I thought I might expire until I heard your planet crying out."

"You're here to destroy us," she dully remarked.

"Hardly destroy. I've learned from my past mistakes. Absolute destruction leads to starvation. Therefore, I shall preserve your planet that it might feed me and make me strong enough to seek out new worlds." The monotone delivery of its manifesto made it all the more chilling.

"When you say feed, you don't mean actually eating people, though?"

The paper body tilted its head and the face crinkled as if it tried to smile. "Nothing so messy. I seek energy. The more chaotic and emotionally charged, the better. What luck humanity has so many different stories that give me exactly what I need."

"You didn't need to curse people for chaos. Our world is already a boiling pot of emotions."

"I can only feed from those that I've linked to what you term the Grimm Effect."

Which explained so much, except for one thing.

"Why were you trying to keep Cinder and Levi apart? I would think that their love would have been a boost if you like emotions so much."

The head definitely grimaced, quite the feat since it

lacked an actual face. "True love is anathema to turmoil and destruction. It is stronger than my compulsion. Poison to my plan."

It sounded dumb, and yet had it just admitted love could defeat this alien invader?

As if it read her mind, the paper body took a step toward her and murmured, "Don't think I haven't seen you thwarting my storylines. You cannot win."

"Don't be so sure of that."

She aimed her wand and lit the paper golem on fire.

1

My first time meeting a prince didn't go so well. I'd been sent to the airport to escort the royal flying in from Corsica, an independent island off the coast of France. I, and a team of Grimm Knights—AKA super agents for the Fairytale Bureau who brought the swords and guns to the fight against curses—waited in the baggage claim area since even our badges couldn't get us past the security checkpoint. Blame the recent fiasco caused by a witch who was peeved an airplane cut off her broom's flight path. She went on a rampage in the airport terminal, turning people into toads.

Since then, security had tightened, hence why we waited for the prince, much to the Knights' annoyance since they took their new mission of protection seriously. I didn't really worry because I knew the prince was arriving with his own set of bodyguards. As for His Royal Highness, I didn't know much about him other than his name, not having had time to peruse the file sent to me by my boss, Hilda. The blame for my lack of preparation rested squarely on the three little pigs who'd run me ragged the night before. I'd been tracking them to try to offer protection from the big, bad wolf determined to eat them. Given how they kept slipping away, I had to wonder if perhaps they might be better off taking care of themselves.

The night before my trek to the airport I'd been hot on their curly tails when they entered the downtown Night Market. I lost track of them in the crush of bodies gathered in front of a temporary stage where some woman in a golden cage sang for a rapt audience.

You'd think three pigs would be easy to spot with their pink skin and tubby bodies. Wrong. The slippery jerks went scooting between people's legs, and let's just say, when I tried to follow, there was much objection. Still, I tried to find them, and when they eluded me once again, I took my disappointment out on some pulled pork.

Savage? Yup. I was okay with it. My patience only went so far, and in my defense, the pork melted in my mouth and made my tastebuds sing.

Anyhow, after that failure, rather than lose more sleep reading a boring file, I slept in as late as I dared before heading to the airport to greet His Majesty. While the Knights watched the perimeter around the baggage claim area, I yawned. Apparently, the prince, despite having access to a private jet, chose to fly commercial. Lovely. One of those out-of-touch entitled pricks who liked to think he was a man of the people.

According to the arrivals board, the plane had landed without mishap and people were clearing customs. As passengers began to exit the glass doors, stiff-legged and weary-looking from the long flight, I kept an eye out for a dude with an armed escort.

Ping.

My phone chirped, and I glanced to see a message from Hilda.

Prince's bodyguards being detained by security for bringing weapons through customs. I'm on the phone yelling at them right now.

I'll bet she was. Hilda didn't have patience for incompetence and someone too big for their britches deciding to cause a diplomatic incident would be enough to push her over the edge.

As the people emerging tapered and the luggage came down to just a few pieces, which were expensive looking and emblazoned with the Corsican royal emblem, a scruffy dude appeared and sauntered over to the conveyer.

I frowned but didn't start moving until the guy reached down to grab one of the royal suitcases. Holy brazen, stealing right in front of me.

I didn't stop to think or even warn. I went into action mode, sprinting the few yards separating us and tackling the guy as he gripped the handle of the luggage.

Thump. We hit the floor hard. Well, he did. I landed on top, snarling, "I don't think so."

The pretty man with shaggy blond hair and brilliant eyes blinked at me. "Um, hello."

"Don't hello me, thief," I snarled.

His lips curved. "I assure you, I wasn't stealing."

"I highly doubt that suitcase belongs to you," my riposte as a Knight finally arrived to render me aid.

Hannah, a tall svelte woman with her hair drawn back in a fat braid, hissed, "Belle, what the fuck are you doing tackling the prince?"

The prince?

My turn to blink. "This is Prince Killian?" Excuse my incredulity. The guy I had pinned to the floor wore a very worn pair of jeans with holes and a T-shirt washed so many times the image on the front had faded.

He had the nerve to grin. "That would be me. And you are?"

"Feeling pretty dumb," I grumbled before adding. "I'm Agent Boucher."

"A pleasure to meet you, Agent Boucher."

"I doubt that," I muttered as I rose from the prince, who kept an amused expression.

Hannah hauled the man to his feet and apologized, of sorts. "Excuse my colleague, Your Highness. She obviously didn't have enough coffee this morning."

"No harm done," the prince magnanimously stated.

"Why are you walking around without your security detail?" I couldn't help a suspicious note. The prince supposedly needed protection, having left Corsica with two bodyguards and been assigned Knights while he visited, and yet here he was, wandering around all la-de-da.

The prince jerked a thumb at the glass doors. "They're still working on reclaiming the weapons the customs people confiscated."

"And you didn't wait for them?"

He shrugged. "I was hungry."

My lips pursed. "They're for your protection."

"So my mother claims." He grimaced. "I find them rather intrusive, especially since no one wants to kill me."

"You're an unmarried prince. You're always in danger." In this world, post-Grimm Effect, eligible royals were few. The fairytale curses being reenacted ensured they either got married, were transformed into a frog, or worse.

"I would give away my rank if I could. Alas, I am my mother's only heir, and so I must suffer the hordes of women who want to become my wife."

"How horrifying," I drawled.

"It is," he agreed. "Do you know how hard it is to weed those with genuine interest from those magically convinced they love me?"

"Poor prince," I taunted. It appeared I couldn't stop myself from being sassy. What could I say? Something about him set me off. It might have been his good looks, his cool, slightly amused composure, or the fact I'd fucked up by laying hands on the person I was supposed to watch out for. Hilda would be pissed, meaning I'd most likely be assigned something worse than chasing pigs.

"Your Highness, we have a vehicle waiting to take you to your hotel," Hannah stated. "And I was told to inform you that the preparations for the ball are well in hand."

"Ball?" I snickered. "Going to find yourself a Cinderella?" My mouth ran faster than my brain.

The remark pursed his lips. "I should hope not. I have no interest in marrying someone who thinks losing a shoe makes her the perfect wife. The ball was my mother's idea, seeing as how I'll be celebrating my fortieth birthday while conducting business."

Forty and single? Impressive. Most princes barely made it out of their teens before they were locked down.

"Here come your guards," Hannah announced as two scowling and burly fellows exited, with the bearded one barking. "Your Highness. You were told to wait with us."

"I'm fine." The prince waved a hand. "My backup security detail has already tackled the job."

Was that a dig?

"Shall we go?" Hannah led the way to the vehicles parked outside, but I didn't ride with the prince. I had my own car here, and as I followed, my phone rang.

Uh-oh, Hilda.

I answered with a cheery, "Hey, boss."

"Don't you hey me. Did you seriously rough up the prince?"

"Hardly roughed up."

"You had him pinned to the floor," her dry reply.

"In my defense, he looked like a vagrant."

"How could you not recognize him? His picture was in the file," she screeched.

"I didn't have time to read it over."

The growling went on for a few seconds before Hilda snapped, "I didn't need this today. I'm already short-staffed as it is, and now, I need to assign someone else to the prince."

"Why? Did he complain?" Pussy, couldn't handle a strong woman and a few bruises.

"No, he didn't, but for the sake of diplomatic relations, I think it's best someone else act as liaison."

"If you insist." I didn't really care. Babysitting a grown-ass man sounded boring. "What do you want me doing instead?"

"You can find those darned pigs," she commanded before hanging up.

Oh, I'd find them all right, and if they caused any trouble, they'd be bacon.

2

After much chasing, and a slog through some mud, I did in fact catch the pigs the day after the incident with the prince.

Despite their squealing, oinking, and farting—oh my god, the farting—I got them to understand I was trying to protect them. Once I promised the pigs all the scraps they could eat, they accompanied me to the Fairytale Bureau where someone would place them in protective custody. As for the wolf... we currently had a Knight hunting him down.

Since I wore a layer of mud head to toe, I chose to head out, but I hadn't quite escaped the building when the prince entered with his entourage.

He looked the same as before, albeit wearing a different shirt. Still very handsome while I looked like

I'd crawled from the sewer. I tried to avoid his eye and keep my head turned as I passed, but he recognized me.

"Agent Boucher. How nice to see you again." Damn him for sounding so cheerful.

I slewed a dark gaze his way and couldn't help saying, "I take it your tushy wasn't bruised from our meeting yesterday."

He smiled wide enough to show perfect pearly whites. "Not one bit. Would you like to take a peek to be sure?"

"I'll take your word for it," I muttered.

"Guess that means no kisses for my boo-boo."

I arched a brow. "I wouldn't advise it, as I've been known to bite."

A deep belly laugh emerged from him, kind of contagious. Had to admire a man who could dish it and take it. "I was dismayed to hear you wouldn't be acting as my liaison," he stated. "And here I thought we'd gotten off to a *smashing* start."

"Why, Your Highness, your file didn't mention your penchant for masochism."

Once more he chuckled. "Then they must have omitted quite a bit, seeing as how I am always getting into scrapes, much to my mother's chagrin."

"How cute you admit to being a mama's boy. Most men have cut the apron strings by your age."

Rather than take offense, he quipped, "What can I say? A bond between mother and son is precious."

Did nothing get under this man's skin? And why was I so determined to rattle him?

"Well, I shouldn't keep you. I'm sure you have important princely things to do."

"If by important you mean avoiding the Cinderellas clustering outside my hotel." He finally showed a hint of a frown.

"Poor little prince has a fan club," I cooed. "Count yourself lucky. My suitors usually have fangs." With that remark, I left. Let him wonder what I meant. I wasn't about to explain that it happened quite literally and I couldn't date because of it.

See, as a young girl, my father inadvertently caused me to be cursed. He travelled quite a bit as a renowned antiquarian, which, for the people about to hunt up a dictionary, was a person who studied really old books. He had access to collections few could imagine. One in particular, owned by a reclusive gent, included a first edition of *Alice in Wonderland*. A favorite story of mine, although it should be noted, as a teenager, I preferred the movie, not the literary version. But my dad, in his excitement, borrowed it to show me. Just one night, but its disappearance was noticed.

The owner of said book had a beastly fit. To

prevent being charged with theft, my father agreed to have me live with the gent as a companion.

Not a sex slave for the pervs who assumed wrong. My task was to read to the owner of the library. Julio, a man in his late twenties, had, almost a decade before, refused to offer succor to an old woman for a night. That old woman turned out to be a witch, and she cursed Julio. He became a beast who roared and snapped and growled, unless someone read to him.

Surprisingly enough, living with Julio didn't prove to be too bad. I lived in a mansion with servants to cater to my needs. I ate very well. Had fine clothes. Even tutors to ensure I graduated high school with honors.

The problem arose when I turned eighteen and Julio asked me to cure his curse. By this point, I'd already become familiar with the Beauty and the Beast storyline, which was one of the few fairytales not from the original Brothers Grimm books. It didn't start appearing until a decade after the other curses started.

Knowing the story, I had to tell poor Julio, whom I'd grown fond of, that, alas, I didn't love him. I mean, the guy was more than a decade older than me, and quite honestly, while nice to me, he could be an ass to others.

He didn't take the rejection well and chose to advise me that his curse didn't require an emotional connection but a physical one with a virgin. I won't horrify with details except to say he attempted to take me by force, while in beast form, and failed.

The heavy book I smashed him with left him stunned long enough for me to flee. When he chased me down the street, running on four paws and roaring, a car running a red light took him out. I'd have felt sadder if it hadn't freed me from the deal he'd made with my father.

Given I'd escaped my curse, albeit under troubling circumstances, the academy that trained the Fairytale Bureau agents recruited me. I'd managed to evade the curse without side effects and was considered one of the lucky ones. Debatable, seeing as how I remained a technical virgin in my thirties because every time I got romantically involved with someone, they turned into a beast.

Every. Single. Time.

It got so that I didn't even bother going on dates anymore. How could I when I knew what would happen? We'd get to know one another. Things would progress to where he'd lean in for a kiss, and wham. Fur, fangs, and growling.

Since love appeared out of reach, I turned to work and books—to my father's delight until he passed a few years ago. I lived vicariously through the romances of others. Read of adventures that took heroines to faraway places in search of treasures and cures to curses. Wished I could be like them.

Alas, I didn't have the resources to go galivanting on quests. Heck, I barely made enough to pay the mortgage and support my book addiction.

As I arrived home, mud flaking from me with every step, I eyed the run-down house I'd purchased for a song. Triple murders had a way of devaluing property. Worked for me. I needed a place with lots of rooms for my books. I entered to their musty scent. Old and new, they lined the walls from the moment you walked in. The bookcases, which I built out of simple pine that I stained, held them neatly lined in rows. Alphabetical by author. Some of them quite rare. All of them read. I didn't hoard books just to own them. I devoured each and every page.

Tonight, though, rather than bury myself in the pages of the newest murder mystery I'd bought, I headed for the turret chamber, a rounded room on the corner of the house that had the least number of books because the walls that didn't have windows held maps instead. A chart of the world with pins that I'd been using to mark where the first instance of each Grimm Effect story reenactment began. I'd color-coded them to differentiate the newer cases from the older, green being the oldest confirmed cases. To my surprise, once I started digging, the green pins clustered only in

England. Also interesting, that British Isle had the most confirmed cases. It hadn't started appearing in North America until a decade later. Europe happened sooner, seeing their first cursed story was within three years of the earliest cases documented.

You must be wondering why I researched this particular fact. Simple, really. I wanted to put an end to the curses. I wouldn't be the first to try, though.

Over the decades since the stories came to life, others had studied the Grimm Effect. Each and every one had been taken out by the curse they sought to eradicate.

Professor Simms wrote papers on the Grimm Effect, hypothesizing that pollution had led to magical side effects. He died when attacked by a flock of swans.

There was an investigative news reporter, Ella something or other. She'd done several pieces outlining the Grimm Effect and how people could protect themselves. She'd been about to depart on a trip to look for the curse origin when got pushed off a rooftop terrace by a murder of crows.

There'd been other incidences of people showing too much curiosity. It led to most being leery of investigating the Grimm Effect.

Not me. I had nothing to lose. Since I couldn't bring myself to have sex with a beast, my lonely existence stretched before me. I had to do something if I didn't want to be alone forever. Yes, I had friends. Yes, I enjoyed my job and I loved my books, but there were times at night, alone in bed, when I really wished I had someone by my side. Someone to hold me. Someone to hug me. Someone to give me an orgasm that wasn't finger or battery-induced.

Blame my horny desire for human touch for my driving determination to solve the Grimm Effect mystery.

Soon, I'd be heading over the big pond to visit a small town where the first case was supposedly reported. I'd been saving up, but not easily. Books tempted me around every corner.

I stood in front of the map and tapped my bottom lip. It had been interesting to note that the first curses definitely originated from the Brothers Grimm stories. Then, about a decade later, we'd begun to see new stories, as well as adaptations of the current reenactments. Then things were steady for a while, for lack of a better term, until recently. Of late, we'd been seeing more fairytales and even nursery rhymes coming to life. The Grimm Effect had expanded. But why, and how did it choose its stories?

I found it odd that it stuck to fairytales for the most part. Why not horror novels or even epic fantasy? Not to say I wanted *IT* by Stephen King to become reality or for the *Lord of the Rings* to turn part of the planet into Mordor. But it seemed strange to me the choice of stories being reenacted over and over around the world. More worrisome, we'd been seeing the curses get darker. More violent.

For example, recently, my friend Blanche Hood, caught up in the Little Red Cap story, had been targeted by a serial killer who left a trail of bodies before trying to murder her. One of the most horrifying cases I'd seen, and it turned out the huntsman was the culprit and not the wolf. We'd seen the rats eat the pied piper. People hunting and roasting the swan princes. The level of violence related to the stories had been rising. It made me wonder just how bad things would get if something wasn't done.

Would I find the answers in England? Maybe. Maybe not. But I would try.

I popped out after a shower to grab some food. A guy leered at me on my way into the sandwich shop, and on the way out, the same fellow started sprouting fur and growling, "Pretty lady want to fuck?"

"No thanks."

When the furry beast ignored my no, he got a taser to the nuts. It dropped him like a rock and left the man, in shreds of his clothes, whimpering on the ground. Maybe that painful jolt would be enough to keep him from transforming again.

I headed home, ate my sandwich, read a book, and,

oddly enough, thought about Prince Killian when I went to bed. It might have been fun working with him. But, no, instead, Cinder got roped into acting as liaison, which surprised. As a Cinderella, she was the one person who should have been kept far away.

I spent the next few days dealing with a variety of oddities such as the bridge that suddenly fell down. Talked to witnesses who claimed they'd seen cows jumping over the moon and that their dishes and spoons were missing. The hospital dealt with a rash of burned bottoms as a bunch of boys chose to jump over candlesticks. Then there was the woman's body found stuffed inside an oversized pumpkin shell. We had a warrant out for her husband Peter's arrest.

The whole world was going mad, and it never became more evident than at the prince's ball, which Hilda declared mandatory for all agents.

Or, as she said at the briefing, *"It's going to be a fucking madhouse. We've got hundreds of Cinderella potentials, one prince who doesn't want to get married, and confirmation that rejection sometimes leads to storyline divergence."* Which was when a grimpher—the name for someone caught in a curse—had their story shift from one angle to another.

All agents had to attend wearing appropriate attire for a ball. In my case, a dress. Ugh. I dug one out of my closet after I moved a stack of books. Unlike Cinder, I didn't have any mice to do my hair or a fairy godmother to glam me up. Good. I wasn't looking to draw attention. Hopefully, I could tuck myself into a corner and read, a hope dashed as I got a taste of the chaos unfolding outside the hotel.

Hilda hadn't exaggerated about the crowd. I couldn't get through at the front of the hotel because of the mob of wannabe princesses wearing massive ballgowns. Cinderella fever had gripped hundreds of women who all clamored to be Prince Killian's wife. I mean the guy was cute and nice, but still, who wanted to marry a stranger?

Once I got inside the hotel, via a tunnel that went from the hotel's laundry into the hotel itself, I found said prince looking ill at ease in a uniform. White with gold braid, very formal and royal looking, if you liked that type. He had my good friend Cinder by his side, who appeared nervous and kept glancing at Levi, the head Knight who stood at the back of the dais set up for the occasion. The other Knights glowered around the ballroom, while the agents from the bureau chatted amongst themselves.

Me, I went looking for a quiet corner to read before the madness started. I'd no sooner cracked my book than the air went electric and, poof, a woman stood before me, looking every inch the Good Witch

Glinda. Wait, wrong story. This had to be the fairy godmother.

"Wrong woman," I stated, only briefly sparing her a glance. "The Cinderellas you're looking for are outside."

"I'm aware. I'm here for you."

That caught my attention. "Why?"

"Because you are not dressed for the occasion. We can't have that," the fairy godmother sang.

"I'm fine." My simple cocktail dress had served me well for a decade now. No point in wasting money on a new one when I hated formal events.

"An important day like today one needs to look her best," she declared.

"First off, not my important day. Secondly, no thanks. I think I already look pretty good."

"Not for what's going to happen."

I closed my book and stood to say, "What exactly is going to happen?"

"A wedding," she exclaimed.

"So the prince chooses a bride. Whoopee." What did I care? And why did I clutch my book so hard my nails dug into the cover?

"Oh, he's not going to choose so much as need an escape. When the time comes, you'll have to give him a sign."

I frowned. "What are you yapping about? What sign?"

"You'll know what to do," she sang. "Together you'll make things right. At least for tonight. And then, you have to come find me."

"Find you where?"

"You already know, and we are running out of time. The ball is about to begin!" She flourished her wand and *kazaam*! To my disgust, I went from wearing a classic little black dress to a gown of shimmering gold. Tight in the waist, too low cut for my taste, with a skirt that swirled around my ankles. And hold a second... A hand to my upswept hair indicated I had roses for a crown.

Ugh. So girly, but I couldn't do a thing about it. The fairy godmother poofed out of sight as quickly as she'd arrived, leaving me uncomfortable and wondering what the heck she meant with her strange comments.

Given her claim of the ball starting soon, I headed back to the main room, where everyone remained on high alert. The prince appeared as if he wanted to flee. Not far from the prince, Cinder glowed, pretty as a princess. She also kept eyeing Levi, making me wonder if the rumors of them being a couple were true.

A rumor confirmed a short time later when the Cinderellas mobbed the ballroom and my friend, rather than marry the prince to stop the madness, proposed to Levi and married him on the spot. Good for her. Or so I thought until the bachelorettes in attendance began clamoring for the prince to choose a bride. Poor sap.

For some reason, I inched closer to the horrified prince and whispered, "You look like you want to run away."

He muttered, "I'd love to, but I don't think I'm going to be allowed to escape without saying I do to a stranger."

"There's always divorce," I replied.

"Indeed," his lackluster reply.

In that moment, a light bulb went off and I remembered Godmother's cryptic message. Surely, she'd not meant for me to marry the prince?

As the Knights ringed us and pushed us back, I lost my grip on my book. It fell, and before I could retrieve it, the prince went on bended knee to reach for it.

I looked at it and then the prince, who had the oddest expression on his face. Wait, was the curse making me into his Cinderella? It would solve his current problem. As for me, this might be my only chance to ever have a fiancé.

"Pick it up," I whispered.

"But—"

"Do you want to marry one of those women?"

He shook his head.

"Then pick it up and pretend so we can get out of here."

The prince offered me a smile of relief and handed over my book saying, "I think this is yours."

"Thank you, dear prince." I pasted the fakest smile on my lips as I replied.

"It is I who must thank you." Killian rose, and I noticed how much taller than me he loomed. He grabbed my hands in his and, in a loud voice that carried, stated, "It would appear I was mistaken in my affection, confused because of how often you were in close proximity, but you, and only you, dear and fair Belle, are my one true love."

"Oh, Killian." To my credit, I didn't laugh as I simpered and batted my lashes.

There was some screaming by disappointed wannabes and then dead silence. Had it worked? Would they believe I was his true love and leave the prince alone?

"If she's really your Cinderella, then marry her, now!"

My eyes widened at the shout, and Killian stiffened.

To his credit, he tried to divert the shrill demand. "We can't have two marriages in one day."

The crowd didn't agree.

"Marry him. Marry him." A chant that grew in volume as the women who'd been jilted insisted on him going through with the farce.

The poor guy looked torn. He'd looked especially torn if the mob turned violent.

What could it hurt? People divorced all the time.

I lifted my chin. "Very well. You want to see me marry the prince, then so be it. If the lady who married Cinder and her Knight would do us the honor?"

The ceremony didn't take long, and I couldn't have said what happened given my state of shock.

In no time at all, I was married to the prince. But the most surprising thing of all?

The jolt of electricity when we kissed.

3

As our lips touched, something sparked. I half expected the prince to turn into a beast. After all, it had happened before with even brief pecks. However, Killian remained human, and even better, the mob of Cinderellas dispersed until only agents, Knights, and the prince remained in the ballroom.

Prince Killian raked fingers through his hair and blew out a breath. "Thank you for saving the evening."

I snorted. "Someone had to do something. Those women would have torn you limb from limb for a piece of you." Heck, they still might. After all, this wasn't a true marriage, merely an emergency measure.

Cinder hustled to my side to exclaim, "Fast thinking marrying the prince! And don't you worry. I'll have it annulled ASAP."

To my surprise, Killian shook his head. "Don't be

too quick." He glanced at me. "If you don't mind, I could use a bit of a respite from having shoes tossed at me."

Being a bit of a smartass, I quipped, "Pity the story wasn't about panties. They'd hurt less."

The chuckle held mirth but also relief. "These past few days have been insane. When did the curse get so bad?"

"Recently," Cinder's flat reply. "We've noticed not only an increase in reenactments but a darker edge to many. It's as if something is agitating the Grimm Effect and it's taken an ominous turn."

"There has to be something we can do," Killian stated. "And before you say it, I know people have been looking—"

I interrupted. "Not really. Most who dared to try and investigate the root of the curse found themselves roped into some of the uglier stories. The kind that don't end well. Needless to say, it's led to a lack of curiosity, as most people don't have a death wish."

"Maybe what happened tonight will put both your stories to bed," Cinder offered.

"Maybe..." I couldn't help a skeptical note.

Killian offered a hesitant, "Do you think so? I'd like to believe it's over, but I do worry an annulment will bring back the madness."

I glanced at Killian. "You know, we could use this

break from the curse to work on cancelling it permanently."

"I thought you said people tried and got punished for it," Killian reminded.

"None of them have been as determined as me, though," I remarked.

"Where would we even start?" Killian asked.

I had a quick reply. "In the town that first reported the Grimm Effect. There has to be a reason it began there and spread. I say we start our search in that area."

"We?" Killian sounded surprised, and yet he quickly nodded. "Yes, let's do it."

"Not alone." Levi showed he'd been listening, despite huddling with his Knights. "Hannah and Gerome will accompany you."

"We will?" Hannah asked in surprise. I'd not even realized she still hovered nearby.

"Yes," Levi stated with a tone that brooked no argument. "You are hereby assigned to the prince and his bride until further notice."

"Aye, aye, boss." Hannah rolled her eyes as she saluted him. As for Gerome, he grunted.

With that command, Levi and Cinder went off to deal with the other Knights and agents, leaving me and the prince alone—if we didn't count the knightly bodyguards.

"Do you think we can find a way to end the

curse?" the prince asked in a wistful tone. "I would do anything to be free to live my life as I choose and not because of some fictional story written down centuries ago."

"We won't know if we don't try."

"Be warned, my mother won't like me gallivanting off."

"Do you always obey your mother?"

His lips curved. "No. Or I'd have been married long before now."

Hannah snapped her fingers. "Save the chitchat for later. We should move somewhere a little more secure in case anyone comes back with vengeance in mind."

"That's my cue to leave. I'll gather my notes and come see you in the morning?" I offered my fake husband.

But it wasn't him that shook his head.

Hannah planted her hands on her hips. "Oh no you don't. You're staying with the prince."

I frowned. "Whatever for?"

"Because you're now the prince's wife and there's a chance not all the women in attendance tonight are free from the curse. One of them might decide to make him a widow."

"How long do I need to be in protective custody?" I grumbled as Hannah glued herself to my side for the walk to the elevator that would take us to the floor the prince currently resided on.

"Until the boss says so. It could be worse. You could be married to a beast," Hannah remarked.

Perish the thought. She did have a point. At least Killian proved to be affable and easy on the eyes. However, I didn't like how my lips still tingled from the kiss. I knew better than to start liking a guy. It wouldn't end well for him.

"Don't be so sure I'm not a beast. I get pretty hangry when I don't get fed regularly." Killian did his best to lighten the restriction on my movement.

"Is now a good time to mention I carry around bear spray?" my sweet reply.

Killian chuckled. "I am not surprised one bit. After all, you've shown yourself to be capable."

"Are you going to whine about that tiny tackle?"

"Tiny?" Hannah scoffed. "You laid him flat."

To everyone's surprise, Gerome muttered, "Good technique."

We arrived at our floor, empty of anyone. Gerome entered the room first and declared it free of intruders—or more accurately uttered a noise that Hannah declared as all clear.

As we entered the room, I eyed the single king-sized bed and small sitting area. The prince had to relocate from the penthouse suite after a dragon attack. I'd not been there when it happened but heard about how a disappointed Cinderella turned into the massive reptile and smashed its way out of the building.

Guess I wasn't the only one with a monster problem.

"I'm starving," the prince declared.

Hannah rolled her eyes. "What a surprise."

"What about you?" His Highness asked, glancing at me.

"I wouldn't mind a snack."

"On it," Hannah stated. "Don't leave this room."

She'd no sooner left than Gerome parked himself in a chair to watch over us.

The prince shook his head. "While I appreciate your attentiveness, do you mind giving me and my bride a moment alone?"

Bride?

Gerome grunted, his usual loquacious answer to everything, and stepped into the hall, but he ensured the door only partially shut by slipping the security bar over the doorframe to keep it from closing fully. Guess that was all the privacy we were getting.

The prince appeared nervous and tucked his hands behind his back, still looking very regal in his white-and-gold-trimmed uniform.

"I never did properly thank you for saving me at the ball."

I waved a hand. "I didn't do it for you but rather to prevent a bloodbath. The Knights would have started shooting if things got out of hand, and that would have been a PR nightmare."

"I still can't believe how insane things got." He rubbed his jaw. "I've been dealing with random Cinderellas since I turned eighteen, but it's never been this bad."

"As Cinder said, things are getting crazier by the day."

"You really think we can find a way to stop the curse?"

"I don't know," my honest reply, which led to his lips turning down. "But I have been studying the Grimm Effect for some time now. Not the stories themselves, or how to alleviate the side effects of people stuck in them, but where they originated."

"Because if we find the root, perhaps we can, if not destroy it, at least contain it and stop it from spreading," he murmured.

"Exactly. And interesting fact, it didn't begin in London like so many assume."

"Wait, it didn't?"

I shook my head. "It took me a while to realize that, while London appeared to be the first to make mention of it, in truth, the very first cases happened in a small town in the countryside. Not common knowledge because, as mentioned, people stopped looking into the origin because of the bad luck that followed."

"You mentioned those seeking out the curse got dragged into badly ending stories."

I nodded. "Indeed, they did, but here's an interesting tidbit. People are only ever roped into one story at a time."

"And how does that help?"

I smiled at him. "Because you and I are already characters. You as the prince for Cinderella, me as the heroine in *Beauty and the Beast*. As such, if we dig into the Grimm Effect—"

"The curse might not like it, but it can't cast us into another tale and try to kill us."

"Oh, it will still try and stop us. Of that, I have no doubt, but it will have to come after us using new methods because, if we stay married, then we're not eligible to Cinderellas or beasts."

His lips pursed. "Unless one of us dies."

"Which I wouldn't recommend."

He snorted. "I'll do my best. Back to the origin of the first curses. I have to ask. Why haven't you already poked at the location you suspect is the root cause?"

"Because I don't have the funds to finance the trip." The honest truth.

"But I do."

My lips twisted. "I'm aware even asking you is a faux pas, but—"

The prince cut me off. "Not rude at all. We both want the same thing. The ability to live our lives. You have the knowledge; I have the money. I think working together is a fine idea."

His eagerness led me to give him warning. "It will be dangerous."

"More dangerous than what we just experienced?" he asked with an arched brow.

"Quite possibly. The Grimm Effect will do its best to stop us."

"It has been doing its best to control me almost my entire life."

"We might not find anything."

"Better to have tried than do nothing at all."

"So you're in?"

He nodded. "Indeed I am, wife."

Despite the spurt of pleasure I felt at him saying it, I grimaced. "Ugh. Can you not call me that?"

"Then what should I call you because Agent Boucher seems a little formal."

"My first name is Annabelle, but my friends call me Belle."

"And I am Killian."

"Which is a mouthful. Don't you have a nickname?"

He shook his head. "Mother never allowed any. She called them disrespectful to a future king."

"Which is bullshit." I slapped a hand over my mouth. "Sorry."

"Don't apologize for speaking honestly. It is bullshit, but…" He shrugged. "Welcome to life as a royal."

"Thank goodness, I'm not a royal," I said with a laugh.

"Hate to break it to you, but as long as we're married, you're now Princess Annabelle."

"But I don't want to be a princess," I hotly declared.

"It's not so bad so long as you don't mind a lack of privacy." He glanced at the partially open door.

"So how much longer are you in town?"

"I can leave anytime now that the ball and negotiations are over. My jet is already fueled and ready to go. I just need to give my pilot a location."

My brows lifted. "Wow, you're really on board with this."

"It's past time someone did something about the Grimm Effect, and you're the first person I've met who understands we need to do more than mitigate the side effects."

"What about your mother, though?" Given what he'd hinted thus far, I doubted she'd be on board with her precious son gallivanting off into danger.

His lips curved. "Mother doesn't need to know our wedding is a sham. As a matter of fact, she'll probably be delighted I've decided to fly my new bride somewhere for our honeymoon."

He'd come up with the perfect cover story.

"In that case, I simply need to get changed out of this dress and pack a few things before we go. Say, two hours?"

At my eagerness, Killian shook his head. "Not so quick. If we're to fool the curse and world at large, we'll need to at least make a pretense this marriage is real, which means we can't leave this room until the morning."

I arched a brow. "You expect me to sleep with you?"

"Of course not!" He hastened to add, "And to ensure your comfort with the ruse, you can have the bed. I'll take the couch." A couch that would force him into a tiny ball given its short length.

My gaze strayed to the king-sized bed. "I'm sure we can both manage to sleep on that giant mattress. No point in you being sore in the morning. After all, it is your birthday." The whole reason for the ball being Prince Killian turned forty on this trip.

He laughed. "And what a birthday it's been."

"You seem awfully good-humored given events."

He shrugged. "What would being sulky or angry

accomplish? I find life much easier to handle if I keep a positive attitude. Although that might not last if I don't get some food."

Luckily, Hannah returned with a bag of fast food comprised of burgers, fries, and even milkshakes.

As we ate with our bodyguards, I related my research and theories, of which I had a few.

"You think someone uncovered something, à la Indiana Jones, and activated the curse," Killian summarized when I finished talking.

"It makes the most sense. Magic didn't really exist before the Grimm Effect. Werewolves, dragons, and the rest either."

"If that were true, then why the many stories?"

"Because people are imaginative."

"And you think some unearthed object brought those fantasies to life?"

"It's one theory."

"Guess it's no worse than the guy who claimed aliens were behind it," Killian stated with a laugh.

By the time we both started yawning, we'd formed an amicable rapport, which turned into nervousness as he pulled back the covers on the bed.

Hannah had been kind enough to loan me shorts and a T-shirt to sleep in, and the prince wore track pants and a T as well. But that wasn't the reason for my agitation. Because of my beast issues, this would be my first time ever sleeping with a man.

True to his word, Killian acted the perfect gentleman who stayed on his side of the bed. He even put a pillow in the middle so he wouldn't encroach on my space.

Turned out it wasn't him that should have worried. When I woke in the morning, I found myself splayed across his chest.

4

Shocked at finding myself snuggling the prince, I flung myself away as if he were lava. Not quickly enough judging by the heat racing through my veins.

"Sorry," I mumbled, cheeks hot with embarrassment.

Killian, on the other hand, appeared amused. He lay on the bed and tucked an arm under his head. "Why apologize? I thoughts wives were supposed to drool on their husbands."

I drooled? I almost wiped my mouth before I realized he teased.

"Not funny," I muttered.

"Are we having our first marital spat?" He arched a brow. "And the honeymoon's not even begun."

"Good thing you have a career as a prince, as you'd

make a terrible comedian," I grumbled without real heat.

His lips curved and I was struck anew by his handsomeness. I glanced away. I had no business admiring Killian. Not only was this marriage a sham but I couldn't risk infecting him with my curse. I had no idea if being married had nullified the beast effect I had on the men I found myself attracted to. I'd rather not find out. His mother might declare war if I ruined her baby boy.

I headed to the bathroom to brush my teeth, wash my face, and pee. I eyed my overnight ensemble with a grimace. I couldn't exactly be seen with the prince dressed as a slob. The golden gown I'd removed the night before hung on the back of the door, only it had returned to the simpler version I'd donned. One problem solved. Fancier than my usual daywear but most likely perfect for my first public outing with the prince.

My husband.

A shiver went through me. While my mind understood the sham of our marriage, another part of me, the part that yearned for a happily ever after with someone, couldn't help a tingly thrill whenever I thought of Killian.

He's not meant for me. Killian deserved to find love with a princess or at least a lady of his rank, not some nobody who felt more at home with books and tended to turn her romantic interests into hairy beasts.

I emerged from the bathroom to see the prince had dressed casually in his usual attire of worn jeans and an old but clean T-shirt.

"I'm feeling underdressed," he observed, eyeing my outfit compared to his own.

"It's all I had. I'll change when I get to my place."

"So we're still going ahead with our plan?"

"If you're still good with it." At his nod, I added, "When do you want to leave?"

"Anytime you're ready."

"I just need to run by my house first to grab my stuff."

"We'll go together after breakfast."

The prince enjoyed his meals, the unhealthier, the better, in his mind. We grabbed some drive-thru from McDonald's, a coffee and muffin for me, but he went all out with an egg McMuffin, hashbrowns, pancakes... As I watched him chowing it down in the back seat, I had to marvel at how he managed to remain slim enough to fit into his uniform.

"How do you not get chunky eating so much junk?" I asked as he polished it off.

"Running his mouth," was Hannah's commentary from the front. Gerome grunted in agreement from the driver's seat.

Killian laughed. He did that often. "Good metabolism and lots of cardio, usually from evading bachelorettes."

"Now that we're hitched, guess you'll be letting yourself go."

"And disappoint my new wife? Never!" he exclaimed, taking the pretense all the way, even in front of our assigned security detail. The first words out of his mouth when Hannah had arrived were, *"Hope we didn't keep you up last night."*

To which she replied, *"No, that would be Levi and his bride."*

I almost cheered. Good for Cinder. She deserved to be loved by someone who didn't suggest putting out rat poison to get rid of her mice. That fellow had an unfortunate string of run-ins with agents after she'd told us of his suggestion. You didn't mess with my friends.

The ride to my house proved uneventful, if we ignored the three blind mice that darted across the road.

Gerome parked in my driveway, and Killian whistled. "Good thing I know what story you're a heroine from, or I'd think you were a witch."

"Who says I'm not? And what's wrong with my house?" Sure, it kind of looked like the one from *Amityville Horror*, and the clapboard siding could use a scrape of the peeling paint and a fresh coat, and maybe the garden needed a bit of weeding, but... Okay, so he had a point. My house did appear kind of spooky.

"I'll check the perimeter," Hannah announced. "Gerome, keep the royals out of trouble."

"I can see she won't be any fun." Killian shook his head as Hannah took off to walk the side and back yard.

"Hannah is a good Knight." Gerome spoke more words than I was used to in one shot.

"Oh, she is, no question about that. A little too good," Killian complained.

"Poor prince can't gallivant about causing trouble," I quipped.

"Ha, if you call trouble me going bowling or mountain climbing. Haven't been able to do much these past few years. The Cinderellas seem to find me wherever I go."

Kind of like me and the beasts. It got to the point I rarely interacted with the opposite sex.

It didn't take Hannah long to scout the outside, and then after grabbing my key, she went inside my house to check for intruders.

Only when she popped out to give the all-clear did Gerome let us out of the car. We walked inside, and Killian uttered a noise. "Your home is a library."

My cheeks turned hot as I mumbled, "I like to read."

"A lot," he stated. "I'm surprised you have time for anything else."

I almost said, like what? I worked, ate, slept, and read. That was my entire life since I couldn't date. I did have some friendships, Cinder and Blanche being my best friends, but we were past the age of partying at clubs and more of the let's-get-in-our-pjs-it's-after-eight. Did I love my life? No. The loneliness, especially at night, alone in bed, overwhelmed, but it beat the other option.

"I take it you're not into books?" I queried.

"Do comics count? I'm a big fan of Archie."

I didn't recoil, but it came close.

The man chuckled. "No need to look so horrified. I like the lightness of cartoons after a day spent dealing with politics. While Mom might still be queen, she's been training me to take over since I graduated university."

"Big job."

He sighed. "It is, and while I love Corsica, sometimes it feels like a prison."

I pointed to the stairs. "I'll pack a bag and gather my notes. Feel free to wander. Maybe you'll find a book with words that intrigue."

"Perish the thought," he exclaimed, giving an exaggerated look of horror. He tucked his hands behind his back and wandered into my living room with Gerome on his heels.

Hannah shadowed me as I trotted up the stairs and headed for my bedroom. I entered and beelined for the closet, only to realize I didn't have a proper suitcase. I'd never actually travelled. I might have stuffed my things in a plastic bag until I saw my bureau-assigned case sitting by the dresser. I'd not brought it to the ball because I hated lugging it around.

It didn't take long to dump it out—vampire stake, holy water, silver cord, salt, candles, and various other emergency items given to all the agents—most of which were useless. Despite that, we were supposed to have our cases with us at all times, but most tended to tuck a single weapon onto their person and leave the oversized suitcase behind.

My nape prickled as I shut and latched the suitcase, leading me to whirl around, expecting to see Hannah. The doorway remained empty. Odd. I poked my head out of my room to see Hannah down the hall, standing watch at the top of the staircase.

I exited, lugging my suitcase, and headed to my investigative chamber next. I wondered what the prince would have thought of my research. Then again, why would I care?

While I had most of my notes saved in files

uploaded to the cloud, I couldn't be sure I'd have internet access where we'd be going, so I took some pictures of a few things. My map on the wall with all the green pins, the color I'd chosen for the earliest confirmed curses, plus some notes I'd been compiling comparing the earliest Grimm tales to later adaptions, pinpointing differences so as to weed out the versions that didn't show up until later.

As I flipped through my notebook, taking images, the sensation of being watched returned. A glance around showed no one there, and yet I couldn't help but feel ill at ease. That discomfiture led to me rushing and, in turn, made me clumsy. I somehow tripped on the chair I'd thought tucked under the desk, and I went reeling. My arms windmilled, seeking balance, but my body kept staggering. I hit the edge of my desk hard, and my hand came down on a pushpin.

"Fucking hell." I cursed rather than whine as I plucked the tack from my palm. A bead of blood welled, and I sucked it. Clumsy but no harm done.

Or so I thought until my knees buckled.

5

I found myself in a strange place. Misty and yet, as the fog shifted in patches, I could see color. A green forest, then the white stone of a castle, the brilliant red of an apple in a tree heavy with fruit, the stillness of a blue lake.

Where was I? Had I teleported? I'd never heard of people actually translocating. Did I sleep? Seemed unlikely given I'd just been in my office doing stuff, and yet there was a certain dream-like aspect to my situation.

As I pivoted slowly, trying to figure it out, a figure strode from the mist, a tall person wearing a full-length cloak with a deeply cowled hood.

"Who are you?" I asked. "Where am I?"

"You are in the before place." The voice emerged

soft, neither feminine nor masculine but rather uniform with a lack of inflection.

"What's the before place?"

"Where the stories begin."

The odd reply led to my concluding, "I'm dreaming." Odd because I last recalled being in my home office, wide-awake.

"This is not a dream but a warning. Do not go on this trip."

"Why not?"

"Because it will not end well for you." The statement sounded even more ominous for its flat delivery.

"And who are you to say that?"

"I am what you call the Grimm Effect."

I arched a brow. "You look more like the Grim Reaper. Just missing the scythe."

"You should not mock me."

"Or what? You'll curse me? Sorry, already dealing with it. Don't recommend. Zero stars." I mocked the cloaked figure because, hello, my dream, and I didn't like to be told what to do.

"I won't have the likes of you stopping me," said with dripping disdain.

"That's rich coming from you. After all, you've been screwing with my life," I riposted.

"Your life is meaningless in my grand plan."

"Excuse me? Your plan that can go fuck itself," my vehement retort.

"You will regret your obstinacy."

"No. What I would regret is doing nothing, and the fact you think you can threaten me tells me I'm doing something right." It felt necessary to put that out there just in case I actually talked to the person behind the curse. Could it be a wizard or sorceress? I'd been assuming the blame lay with an object this entire time, as it went with my theory of something being uncovered. However, it could be possible someone stumbled across some kind of spell book or power and started this mess.

"So be it. You've made your choice."

The figure faded, as did the mist and everything else.

I suddenly found myself lying on the floor of my office, with hands pumping my chest rhythmically, but I blinked when a mouth pressed against mine and blew air. Nice lips belonging to a prince, and what did I do?

Nipped Killian's bottom lip before murmuring, "Next time, start with a kiss."

"You're awake." I went from having Killian's mouth to play with to being dragged into his arms for a hug. He gave me a good squeeze and murmured, "You had me worried."

"What happened?"

"I heard a thump and entered to find you passed out," Hannah's flat response.

"You weren't breathing," Killian added.

I pushed out of his embrace and sat up. "Yeah, it was the weirdest thing. One minute, I was taking pics of my stuff, and the next, I was having a weird dream."

"Weird how?" he asked.

Did I tell him? It sounded fanciful even by today's measures. Not to mention, no one had ever claimed to speak to the person behind the curse anymore. More likely, I'd fainted due to all the excitement, and my subconscious had me imagining things because of my anxiety over the quest we embarked upon.

"Most likely just the excitement from the ball caught up to me." I rose and wavered slightly, not enough to fall, and yet Killian was there to steady me.

"Easy," he murmured.

"I'm fine. I'm almost done here. Where's my phone?"

Hannah plucked it from the table with my notes and handed it over. "How much longer are we sticking around?" she asked.

"Just give me a second to change." Because, while I'd packed, I'd not yet swapped my dress for something I could travel in comfortably.

Hannah followed me to the bedroom rather than sticking to the hall. As I rummaged in my drawers, she kept her voice low as she asked, "What really happened?"

I cast her a glance over my shoulder. "What do you mean? I fainted."

"You didn't just faint. You stopped breathing and went cold. The prince freaked."

I lifted a sweater from the drawer and closed it before answering. "In that case, maybe my dream wasn't a dream."

"Explain." Hannah crossed her arms and stared.

"I pricked my finger a few seconds before I passed out, and next thing I knew, I was in some misty place and some person in a cloak told me to not seek out the origin of the curse."

"And you didn't mention this because…"

"For one, it sounds crazy, for two, I have no intention of obeying, and three, I didn't want to worry the prince."

"Doesn't he have a right to know?"

"Know what?" Killian stood in the doorway, and I sighed.

"When I passed out, I had a dream where someone claiming to be in charge of the curse told me I'd regret looking into it."

"Someone threatened you?" Killian's wide-eyed reply.

"I mean kind of. They told me I'd regret it, but I

replied I'd regret more doing nothing. Which is the truth."

"You shouldn't be making light of it," he retorted.

"I can and will because the idea of the curse threatening me is ridiculous. It's much more likely a stress-induced episode."

"And if it wasn't?" Killian insisted.

"No one has ever talked to anyone claiming responsibility for the curse."

"That you know of," he pointed out.

"I'll understand if you want to bow out of the trip." I didn't mention I'd be going anyhow. Time to stop gathering intel and act.

"Like hell. You're not getting rid of me that easily. The fact the curser is worried is all the more reason for us to go."

My turn to try and dissuade him. "It will be even more dangerous now that the Grimm Effect knows we're looking."

"More dangerous than hundreds of Cinderellas with weaponized shoes?"

My lips quirked. "So you're still in?"

"Yup."

I glanced at Hannah. "What about you and Gerome? It doesn't seem fair to drag you along and put you in peril for our quest."

She snorted. "Honestly, this sounds way more fun than hunting some foxes and a noisy hen."

Killian clapped his hands together. "Then we're decided. If you've got what you need, what do you say we take to the skies?"

His eagerness proved contagious.

"I'm ready. Let's go."

We had only a slight delay on our route. As we sat at a red light, a swell of water suddenly washed through the cross street, the wave carrying a large tub with three men inside. One of them faced backwards waving a cane, and I wondered why until a shark emerged to snap its teeth. They passed out of sight, and Killian murmured, "Was that... Did I see..."

"A shark chasing a bathtub? Yes."

As for the water, it dissipated as quickly as it came, and we made it to the small airport without further hindrance. Seeing the jet on the tarmac, I did have a question.

"How is it you have a plane here when you arrived via commercial airline?"

"The jet had some landing gear issues, and I chose to not delay my trip. Mother had it sent once the repairs were completed."

Which led to me asking another question. "Whatever happened to your original bodyguards?" I recalled mention of him having a pair when I'd tackled him at the terminal.

"They got snagged by the Grimm Effect. Tom suddenly shrank to thimble size and ran away before the bureau could capture him. While Horace ran off with the woman who cleaned my suite."

"The curse trying to render you defenseless?" I opined.

"If true, then why weren't the Knights affected?" Killian countered.

"Because they defeated their curses."

"But we know now that some people can get afflicted with a second bout," he reminded.

"Then maybe it's because they're now heroes, fighting injustice, meaning they're still part of the stories?" I spit-balled something plausible.

"Maybe."

"Gerome is going to check on the plane. You two try to not steam up the windows so I can keep an eye on you," Hannah warned before getting out to stand by the car.

"She's not funny," I muttered.

"I don't know. Her brand of sarcasm is unique. Most people are leery of teasing me."

"Afraid you'll scream 'off with their heads'?"

"Don't even mention that story." He shuddered. "Can you imagine if we had a mad Queen of Hearts?"

"I'd hope to meet that caterpillar who smokes the good stuff. He seemed very chill and relaxed."

Killian laughed so hard Hannah popped her head into the car to eye us suspiciously before ordering us out. "Let's go. Gerome says the plane is ready."

Our luggage got loaded while we embarked, the interior a luxury I'd never had the pleasure of enjoying before. Buttery leather seats, the fat and comfy kind that could recline. Two couches that faced each other. Chilled, bottled water. A tray of snacks which Hannah insisted on trying before us in case of poison.

I smirked as I flopped into a chair. "Now this is what I call travelling in style."

"Perfect for our honeymoon," Killian declared. "Although you'll have to forgive me. I forgot to pack my lingerie."

My lips curved. The man did have a better sense of humor than I expected in a royal. "I think you'd look dashing in a black lace teddy."

At the back of the plane, Hannah coughed.

Killian outright laughed. "I'll keep that in mind. Anything I can get you?"

"A prince serving a commoner?"

"A prince should always service his princess."

And he meant it. I didn't have to lift a finger. If my water got low, he replenished. He made sure the snack tray remained full, all the while providing witty banter.

I reclined and sighed. "This is the life."

"Have you ever been married?" he asked out of the blue.

"Nope. Can't. The curse isn't happy I jilted the beast, and since then, any attempts at being amorous are met with a new beast."

"Hold on. Are you saying you don't even date?"

"Not anymore because a single kiss and, bam, suddenly I end up with a hairy jerk who wants to do the horizontal, bestial tango."

"Yikes," he replied, only to add, "We kissed, and I'm still me."

I'd thought about it and come to a single conclusion. "Probably because you're the prince of another story."

"And the curse doesn't like to double up." He nodded. "This town we're visiting... Anything I should know about it?"

"It's not real interesting other than the fact the first confirmed Grimm Effect case started there, although that wasn't known for a decade due to poor record-keeping in the beginning. One Deborah Goodwin woke up and ghsindopliink—" My words suddenly emerged garbled as my mouth twisted violently and my jaw cracked. All of me torqued something odd.

Should I mention it hurt? Like really hurt! Not

that I could scream. My entire being went rigid, and I was momentarily blind.

When the pain subsided, and I spoke, my voice emerged huskier than usual. "That was weird."

"Um, Belle…"

"What?" I asked, eyeing him across from me and wondering at his shocked mien.

"How to say this?" Rather than tell me, Killian held up his phone, and I wondered why until I saw the monster reflected on the screen.

Wait, not just any monster.

The beast with the furry face and mane?

That's me.

6

So, I freaked out a bit.

Okay, a lot.

It didn't help Hannah had her gun out and aimed at my face. It took Killian's sharp, "Put that away," before Hannah lowered it.

And I gave her heck for it. "Don't you dare put your guard down. I could be a threat to the prince."

"You? A threat?" She chuckled. "You're not that ferocious. More like an overgrown kitty."

A big kitty. The beast tended to have lion characteristics. Although, in my case, despite me being female, I did have quite the long and luscious mane.

"What the fuck? Oh my god. Argh."

I might have thrown myself from the plane if not for Killian's remark of, "See what happens when you forget to shave, dear wife."

I stopped losing my mind to gape at him. "This isn't funny. I'm a monster."

"A beast, yes, but monster? Hardly. After all, you still seem to have your wits about you."

"Barely."

"Are you going to try and eat me?"

"No!"

"Pity." He winked.

"Not. Funny." I roared. Like literally.

Hannah's gun-toting hand twitched. Would she shoot me? Most likely yes, if I did something stupid. Then again, I'd do the same in her position.

Suddenly deflated, I sat down hard in my seat. "I don't understand what's happening."

"The curse appears to have chosen to throw you a rather devious curveball."

"This is more than a curveball. It's a slam dunk. I'm hideous." I know it shouldn't matter. I should rise above it all and blah, blah, blah, but I dared anyone to not be a little traumatized going from smooth-skinned to furry, head to toe.

"Bah, are you a little hairy? Yes, but you still have your shining personality, and if I'm honest, you're cute enough to scratch."

I glared at him. "You're not helping."

He shrugged. "What would you prefer I say?"

"I don't know." I slouched.

"Since you're more familiar with this curse than me, how is it usually resolved?"

"By having sex with a virgin."

He choked on his sip of water. Coughed so hard Hannah pounded him on the back.

"This is a nightmare," I groused. "How am I supposed to investigate anything? I'll be picked up by the first agent who spots me."

"Only if you're violent," Hannah pointed out.

"Which tends to happen to most of the beasts after a while due to the constant rejection," I growled.

"Someone's getting hangry. Have another cookie." Killian shoved one in my direction.

I meant to slap it out of his hand. Instead, it ended up in my mouth. The chocolate did soothe me a bit.

"How long before we land?" I asked, hating my new huskier voice.

"It's an eight-hour flight usually. We left early afternoon, but given the time zone changes, by the time we arrive, it will be close to dawn."

"Wake me when we start our approach." I couldn't bear to have anyone staring at me, not while I struggled with this sudden change. I made my way to the couch further down the plane and lay on it, facing the wall, gnashing my teeth.

A blanket dropped over me, and Killian softly said, "It will be all right. I promise."

"You can't promise that," I whispered.

"Oh yes, I can. I am the future king of Corsica, and if I decree it, then so shall it be."

I snorted, not a pretty sound in this shape. "You can't order this curse away."

"Perhaps not, but I can offer solace." I didn't understand what he meant until he snuggled in behind me on that narrow couch, barely big enough for two, but he managed, an arm draped around my middle, his face buried in my mane.

It comforted more than I would have expected. His kindness kept me from collapsing into utter despair. All the times I'd rejected beasts, it never really occurred to me to wonder how they felt.

Not good, as it turned out.

Despite my turmoil, I managed to sleep until Hannah bellowed, "What the fuck do you mean we're being followed by a pod of dragons?"

I sat up so abruptly I bumped Killian off the couch. He hit the floor, and I muttered a quick, "Sorry," before I barked—quite literally—"What now?"

A steely-faced Hannah said, "Dragons. Three of them. Coming in fast. The pilot caught them on the radar."

"And we're sure they're after us?" A dumb question, because, hello, of course they wanted to take us down. The curser had warned me. I just didn't expect this level of malevolence, and yet I should have. Of late, the Grimm Effect had been getting darker and more violent with its stories.

"There's nothing else out here, so I'd say it's a fair bet."

Killian remained sitting on the floor where he'd fallen, wearing a frown. "Has the pilot called for air support?" Countries had fighter jets on standby for the times dragons decided to cause trouble, whether it be planes, crops, or livestock. The larger commercial airlines had taken to even having fighter jets accompany them on overseas flights.

"The radio stopped working a few minutes before the dragons appeared."

"How far are we from land?" I asked. A glance out the windows still showed dark skies.

"Too far," her low reply.

"Does this jet have any firepower?" In today's world full of magical threats, people tended to be more prepared. I'd heard of private jets armed with missiles and machine guns.

Not my prince's ride. "We've got nothing. Mother likes dragons. Says they're misunderstood and so refused to have the plane outfitted with any offensive weaponry."

"Meaning we're screwed if they attack." I rubbed my face. Felt the fur. Tucked my hand by my side.

"It is equipped with life rafts," he offered, as if that were a viable solution.

"That would entail us going down in the ocean. At night. Far from land. Oh, and with dragons able to pick us off from the sky." I pointed out the flaws with his stupid suggestion.

"I have my spear." Gerome had been so quiet up until now I'd forgotten the man. He emerged from the back hefting said weapon.

"Which requires you opening a door. I don't know about you, but my understanding of pressurization and stuff says that would be bad." I'd seen the movies with people sucked out of the plane.

"No opening the door at this altitude." Hannah wagged her finger at Gerome.

"Give 'em a solution, and they still bitch," Gerome muttered, slinking back to his corner.

"Maybe we're panicking for nothing," Killian remarked, glancing out the window. "Could be the dragons are just going in the same direction."

"Your mother should have called you Pollyanna." A character from a book who always brimmed with optimism.

"Guess we'll soon find out." Hannah pointed, and as I looked out the window, I saw a jet of orange fire in the distance.

Not far enough away, I should add.

It should be noted I was a damned good field agent, who'd had to use a taser more than once. I considered myself pretty adept at handling most situations.

On the ground.

In the air, at night, over an ocean?

Screwed. So screwed. And all my fault as well. It had been my idea to go on this trip. My decision to ignore the warning in my dream. Now, everyone on board would pay the price of my stubbornness.

"Jeezus, y'all look like we're already dead when, instead, we should be preparing," Gerome stated. The gruff man took charge. "Hannah, tell the pilot to drop us as low as he can over the water. Prince, you pull the life raft out from under that couch." He pointed. "You"—you being me—"brace yourself and hold on to the prince when I open the door."

"I thought we agreed opening the door was a bad idea." I felt a need to remind.

"At high altitudes, yes, but we'll be low enough the pressure won't be an issue and close to the water if we need to jump." It wasn't the fact that Gerome kept talking that dropped my jaw.

"Jump?" Turned out a beast could squeak.

"Only if the plane runs into trouble." Gerome spoke calmly, as if this were an everyday occurrence.

"You think we're going to crash?" There I went high-pitching again.

"Crash or burn. Could go either way." Gerome pointed to the window and the visible glow emanating from an open dragon mouth. It had gotten close enough for me to see its beady eyes.

Just as the flames began to spew in our direction, the plane dropped, the sudden incline sending me staggering and falling in a very unmonster-like heap by Killian's feet.

"You don't have to throw yourself at me, wifey poo. We're already married," quipped the prince. Did nothing ever shatter his good attitude?

"Don't you have something to do?" I snapped.

"Already done. I've got the boat. Now what?" he asked of Gerome.

"Brace yourselves. It's gonna get bumpy and windy," Gerome stated before turning to bellow, "Hannah!"

"Coming," she muttered, emerging from the cockpit, a gun in hand. "Wished I'd not stowed the rifle in the baggage compartment, though. These puny bullets won't do shit unless I manage to shoot it in the eye."

The plane evened out, and a glance outside showed the dark shimmer of water as the plane's lights danced over the surface.

Now for the moment of truth. Had the dragons followed?

A jet of fire hit the plane on both sides, a sheet of flame that washed over the windows. They didn't melt. It would take more than a short burst to—

Smash.

I couldn't have said what impacted the glass, only that we suddenly had a sucking hole.

"Hold on to the boat," Killian advised.

The suggestion seemed like the best option for the moment, especially as the air turbulence increased when Gerome cranked open the door.

The whoosh of wind blew my mane in my face. I couldn't see much, but I did feel the sudden sear of heat as fire roasted the opening. I slapped a hand to my forehead to hold my shaggy bangs out of my eyes.

Pop. Pop.

A grim-faced Hannah stood braced in the doorway, firing her gun.

"Where's Gerome?" I shouted to Killian.

He pointed outside.

Poor guy must have fallen.

Wrong. A dragon swooped past, a sleek reptile but for the person hugging its back with his knees while holding a spear.

Hot damn.

The duo flew past, and I left Killian's side to peek

out the window just as flames baked it. I recoiled at the heat and felt Killian's hand on me. "Gerome took down one, but there's still two more."

"Where's Gerome now?"

Killian appeared glum as he said, "In the water. He jumped after he stabbed it."

Oh. "Should we toss him the boat?"

This time, Hannah replied. "He's fine. It will take more than a swim to kill Gerome."

Kind of optimistic seeing as how he bobbed in the ocean with dragons circling overhead.

Bang.

The plane wobbled, and my gaze followed Hannah's to the ceiling. *Thump. Thump.*

"We have company," she stated unnecessarily.

"What should we do?" Because I didn't have a single idea. None of my training ever prepared me for this.

Crash.

The pilot screamed, or so I assumed since it wasn't any of us hollering.

"Shit." Hannah bolted for the cock pit but was too late. The plane tilted, and the impact as it hit the water sent me tumbling.

More worrisome than the fact I'd landed in an ignoble heap?

We were sinking!

7

Being dumped into the ocean might be a bad time to regret never learning to swim. As my fur got waterlogged, I struggled to keep my head above the water rising in the plane's cabin. Would drowning hurt?

Apparently, I wouldn't find out today because Killian said, "Don't worry. I've got you."

Indeed, Killian gripped my shirt, the fabric stretched to my changed bulk but holding as he dragged me. I might have blubbered stupidly, but for one, I had to keep my mouth shut to avoid swallowing water, and two, he appeared to have a better plan than dying.

"We're going to have to dunk under for a second to get out," his brief warning before the yank that dragged me below the surface.

It took everything in me to not panic at the submersion. I held tight to my fear, and a moment later, my head cleared the water. I sucked in a breath.

"Hold on to this rope." Killian placed my hand on a nylon cord, attached to the inflatable raft, which he'd somehow managed to keep in all the turmoil. It expanded rapidly, almost snapping me off as it exploded to its full floating size.

Rather than Killian clambering on first, he boosted me, dumping my soggy butt into the swaying lifeboat. When he didn't immediately join me, I scrabbled to peer over the edge.

"Killian?" I was in time to see him diving under the water and entering the sinking plane. A plane that still glowed, as the lights hadn't yet extinguished.

What was he doing? Then it hit me. Hannah remained inside.

I couldn't keep watch to see if he succeeded in his rescue, as a flap of wings drew my eyes overhead. The remaining pair of dragons still circled!

One swooped for the raft, opening its maw, getting ready to roast me. The whole raft rocked, and I thought it would capsize, only it steadied as a soaked Gerome suddenly appeared, throwing himself into the boat, spear in hand. The maniac didn't stay, though. He launched himself into the air just as the dragon swooped low to barbecue my butt. The point of his weapon entered the dragon's mouth, and it squealed as it thrashed its head side to side. Despite its vigorous protest, it couldn't dislodge the spear or the man holding it. Gerome swung like a pendulum with each shake.

The pair crashed into the ocean, the impact sending my raft away from the airplane. Of Hannah and Killian, I could see no sign. But the third dragon?

Yeah, it was swooping and bugling as it came right at me. Damn it. Exactly how many close encounters with death would I experience in one night?

The dragon skimmed low across the water, the lightening horizon showing dawn not far away. Not that sunlight would help, and all I had to defend myself? A plastic oar.

I could have cowered. Sobbed. All reasonable actions given the situation, but while terror did grip me, I realized I couldn't afford to be a shivering pussy if I wanted to live. Being brave came with lots of screaming as I launched myself into the air. As the dragon went to spew fire, I whacked it on the nose with my oar.

To no effect, I should add, but in good news, you know what doesn't burn when sopping wet?

Fur.

I got warm, uncomfortably so, but I didn't light on fire or burn to a crisp. Luckily, I landed back in the boat, still with my battle oar. The dragon had swept past, but I figured it would probably come back around.

The boat rocked as Gerome heaved himself on board still holding his spear. I almost wondered how he managed to retrieve it until I saw the cord tethered between the weapon and his wrist. Smart.

He held it ready, but the remaining dragon decided to value its life and flew off, leading Gerome to mutter, "Coward." Only he would be disappointed.

With the dragon no longer imminently threatening, I yelled, "Killian went back into the plane for Hannah."

Gerome glanced at me then the water. He sighed. "She hates being saved," he muttered before readying to dive in.

He didn't jump, most likely because two heads popped above the surface.

I couldn't help but smile in relief, my joy at seeing them both as bright as the cresting sun. Speaking of which, its rays hit me and so did discomfort and crackling. And did I mention pain?

Not again. Would I turn into something worse than a hairy feline beast?

Instead, hair sank into flesh.

My flesh.

I held up my hand and grinned. I was normal again!

Hooray.

A hooray that doubled when Killian clambered aboard, along with Hannah.

We'd survived. Although our poor pilot hadn't.

I threw my arms around Killian and hugged him tight.

He squeezed me back and murmured, "I'm happy to see you too."

My excitement at surviving proved short-lived as a scowling Hannah, hands planted on her hips, surveyed the undulating waves and said, "We are so fucked. Ain't no way we're making it to shore in this dingy."

Killian shook his head and smiled. "Don't be so sure of that." He glanced at me. "I'm going to do something to get us out of this mess. Try to not be jealous."

"Um, jealous of what?" His statement made no sense.

"You'll see."

I rolled my eyes. "Now is not the time to be mysterious. If you have a solution to our dilemma, spit it out."

"You know I'm a prince, right?"

"And?" I huffed. "Not exactly the time to remind us of your title."

"That title is going to save us. Now excuse me while I emasculate myself calling for help." Killian stood on the prow of our little boat and bellowed, "Marina, it is I, your sweet prince. Where art thou, beautiful songbird of the sea?"

My brow arched, and I could see Hannah equally confused. Gerome sat with his spear in his lap, watching the sky. Should have been watching the water.

The tentacle poked up from the waves, and I swear it peeked at us, given how it turned left and right as if scanning the entire boat.

"Um, Killian...." I spoke softly and wondered if he heard me over his singsong chant that used the word Marina and beautiful a few too many times.

"What is it?" He glanced at me, and I pointed.

He saw the tentacle, and the psycho grinned. "It won't be long now."

"Won't be long before what? We're octopus food?"

"You'll see." He sounded entirely too cheerful.

A fish burst from the water, arcing in the dawn light, its tail sleek and shimmering, the iridescent scales catching the sun's rays. As it rotated in the air, it spread its arms, and its hair spun away from its torso, revealing breasts!

I gaped at the mermaid as she splashed back down.

She soon reappeared and hoisted herself on her forearms to cling to the side of the boat.

"Sweet prince," she gurgled. "You called for me."

"Indeed, I did. My companions and I find ourselves adrift with no clue as to where to find shore."

"That way." A tail flicked from the water, showering us with droplets.

"Very helpful, thank you," Killian stated. "However, we also find ourselves without a motor or a sail."

"You have two legs. You could always kick." Her laughter emerged like water running and babbling over rocks.

"I don't suppose you could help us?"

A sly expression crossed Marina's face. "I could, but it will cost you."

"And what would you ask of me, my beautiful sea siren?" Killian asked with a smile that probably dropped panties—and shoes—when unleashed. I know if he'd turned it on me, I might have been tempted.

"You know what I want, sweet and sexy prince," Marina said on a coy note, her tail slapping the surface of the water. "You."

My brows just about hit the atmosphere at her obvious suggestion.

"Alas, we are still not compatible in that respect." He sounded chagrinned, and I had to wonder if he truly felt that way because, while half female, Marina still appeared rather alien with her seaweed-like hair, her black unblinking eyes, and her pearly moist skin.

"A shame indeed. I guess I shall have to settle for a kiss." Marina pursed her lips, plump and dark green.

"One kiss," he stated, "and you will bring us safely to shore."

"One proper kiss," she corrected, parting her lips to show sharp teeth like a shark's.

"Agreed." He leaned down, and to my shock, I felt a spurt of irrational jealousy. I knew he did it to save us, and it was just a kiss, but...

He's my husband.

In name only, but still, it bothered me to see him with his mouth pressed to another.

It lasted mere seconds—an eternity—and Marina flipped away, literally. In and out of the water, bouncing all over. I began to think she'd duped Killian, only the tentacle poked its tip through a loop of rope on our boat, and suddenly we were skimming and bouncing over waves.

I held on, all I could do since I didn't want to get tossed. I doubted Marina would have her pet octopus turn around to save me.

Killian sat down and didn't look at me. Was he thinking of the mermaid? Wishing they were compatible?

Hannah whooped. "Yee-haw! This is better than tubing."

As for Gerome, he napped.

Killian reached for my hand and laced his fingers with mine. He still hadn't said anything, but it oddly comforted. I leaned my head on his shoulder and actually fell asleep. I couldn't tell how long we travelled, only I woke at Hannah's shout of "Land ho!"

And apparently, the end of our ride.

The tentacle disappeared, and we rolled into the rocky shore with the incoming tide.

We'd survived the night.

But I now had to wonder if we'd live to see the next.

8

Slogging ashore, we must have looked quite the sight. Bedraggled, me in my stretched clothes, Gerome with his spear, and Hannah clomping in her water-laden boots. It probably explained why we were met at the top of the bluff by a pair of Fairytale Bureau agents.

"Stop right there!" shouted a portly fellow with an impressive mustache.

Hannah didn't listen and strode for the mustache man and his female companion with the buzz-cut blonde hair.

"I said halt." The man pulled his weapon, and Hannah, without missing a step, spun her foot and knocked it from his hand.

"None of that," she snapped. "It's been a long night. I'm Grimm Knight Hannah, and this is my partner, Grimm Knight Gerome." Funny how none of the Knights ever used a last name. I'd heard rumor it was because of their initiation, which had them cast their past lives aside.

The blonde agent kept her hand on the butt of her gun. "If you're a Knight, then prove it."

Hannah dug into her soggy pocket and pulled out her metal badge. "Satisfied? Good," she stated before the agents could reply. "I'm going to require transportation and accommodation."

"Just a minute. Who are these two?" The mustache agent pointed at me and Killian.

I swear Hannah looked absolutely feral as she bared her teeth and stated, "This is the Crown Prince of Corsica and his wife. Now, are you going to start moving your asses, or do I need to escalate with someone higher up? I'm sure the Queen of Corsica will be delighted to hear how you're treating her son. Not to mention, the diplomatic issues that will mostly arise, given his plane was attacked by three dragons that came from your coast."

"And you survived?" the blonde blurted out with surprise.

"Not all of us. Our pilot didn't make it."

"I'm surprised the dragons didn't finish you off." Mustachio didn't get the hint to not screw with Hannah.

"Bah. I killed two of them, and the third chose to not stick around to join them." Gerome's claim widened their eyes.

"Uh. We won't all fit in the car," Mustachio stammered.

"We will. You won't. We're confiscating your vehicle. Call someone to pick you up." Hannah held out her hand and waited.

The blonde didn't argue, simply dropped the keys into her waiting palm.

"I'll drive. Your Highnesses will sit in the back." Hannah marched off, but Killian paused a moment to say, "Corsica thanks you for your aid."

Rank did have some privilege, and I might have felt bad at stranding the agents, but the warmth inside the car did much to dispel my shivering, as did Killian's arm around my shoulders tucking me into his body.

"Where are we going?" he asked as Hannah sped away from the beach.

She glanced at Gerome. "Where's the nearest hotel?"

The man had his phone out, the waterproof case having survived his dunk in the sea. "No hotel. There's a safe house on the outskirts of Padstow. It's not too far from here."

Hannah glanced at us in the rearview mirror. "Safe

house it is, then. We can rest and re-equip ourselves while planning our next move."

"Our next move is heading to Ashbrittle." I reminded them of our destination. "How far is the safe house from it?"

"A couple of hours," Gerome muttered.

"Shouldn't we just drive there directly?" A few hours meant we were close.

"We were just attacked by dragons. So, no, we are not heading there, not until we've had a chance to load up on weapons, eat, and change out of these wet clothes. If the curse is trying to foil us, we'll probably face another attack soon." Hannah pointed out the obvious, and I could have kicked myself for not thinking clearly.

"We'll also need to contact my mother before she sends out an army to look for me," Killian added.

"Of course, Your Majesty," Hannah replied.

"Please, I think we've been through enough that you can call me by my first name."

Hannah inclined her head. "If you insist."

"Speaking of being through a bunch of stuff, anyone else hungry?" Killian asked.

I tilted my head to stare at him. "Seriously?"

He shrugged. "What can I say? All that commotion gave me an appetite."

"We are not stopping for food. We'll fetch something once we reach the safe house." Hannah didn't give in to his bottomless stomach.

Safe house proved to be a misnomer, seeing as how we pulled to a stop in front of a castle. "This is where we're hiding? A castle doesn't seem too subtle." I couldn't help but speak my mind.

"We don't need subtle, we need secure, and it's a manor house, not a castle," Hannah corrected.

Maybe to her, but to my American brain, the massive stone edifice sure seemed impressive.

We arrived to find the main doors closed, but I spotted movement on the roof. Someone aimed a rifle in our direction, but the Knights didn't seem bothered by it.

Hannah waved. "Hey, Clive."

"Hannah, is that you?" a man shouted.

"In the soggy flesh. Got room for the crown prince of Corsica and his wife?"

"He's alive?" Clive exclaimed. "Jeezus, his mother has been lighting up all the emergency channels looking for news of him since the jet lost contact."

Killian glanced at me. "Told you so."

"Mama's boy," I muttered in reply.

"I'm coming down." Clive disappeared from the roof and, in short order, led me and the prince to a massive bedchamber, with one bed, but I ignored that fact in favor of the hot shower, which Killian insisted I use first while he contacted his mother. I didn't argue. Terrible water pressure, and not as scorching as I would have liked, but it did much to dispel the clammy from my skin.

I emerged wearing an oversized towel to find my husband, er, Killian, lying sprawled on the bed, a cell phone to his ear.

"No, Mother. I already told you I'm not coming home yet." He glanced at me and rolled his eyes. "I am not cutting my honeymoon short."

He'd obviously not told her of our mission.

"My wife is fine. We are both uninjured and eager to get started on making you the royal babies you keep bugging me for."

While I knew he said that to placate his mom, my cheeks still heated.

"No, I don't need you to come join us. I'm afraid we'd be poor company, as I have no intention of us leaving the room for anything other than food."

My face burned even hotter.

"Love you too, Mother. Bye." He sighed as he hung up.

"That sounded like fun."

"My mother loves me a tad too much. Do you need to call someone?" He offered the phone.

"I've got no family. My mother died when I was born, and Dad passed a few years ago."

"Sorry to hear that."

I wrinkled my nose. "Don't be. My dad and I weren't close. I mean he did his best, but his idea of caring for me involved cutting my hair very short since he hated brushing it, handing me money to buy my own clothes, and forgetting to make us dinner because he got lost in some ancient book. As for not having a mom"—I shrugged—"hard to miss what I never had." Not entirely true. I'd often wistfully wondered what it would have been like.

"My mom was the opposite and meddled in everything about my life, if from afar."

"Too busy ruling Corsica," I surmised.

"That was only part of it. While overseeing the kingdom kept her occupied, she always found time to talk to me every day. At a young age, she had me shipped to a farm so I could have a normal childhood. I went to public school, on foot, I should add. I did chores around the farm. It wasn't until I graduated from university that I got dragged into the palace drama."

"But you knew you were a prince growing up?"

"Yeah, that was never a secret from me, just my classmates and their parents. At the time, I didn't really think much about it."

"And now?"

"Kind of wish I could go back to being a farmer.

There is something satisfying about planting crops and harvesting. Of milking a cow for fresh milk." A wistful tone hued his statement.

"I guess your upbringing explains your love of casualwear."

He glanced at himself, currently wearing a navy blue track suit that he must have borrowed. "Regular clothes are more comfortable than a suit or uniform. With jeans and cotton shirts, there's no one nattering at you for the wrinkles in your pants or the stain on your shirt."

I cocked my head. "I don't suppose you grabbed some extra clothes for me?" I still hugged the towel around my body.

"I am such a cad. Yes." He sprang from the bed and strode to a chair with a pile. "The sizing won't be great, but they're warm."

I returned to the washroom to change into the oversized garments and emerged to find him chatting with Hannah, also dressed in a track suit. A tray laden with dishes sat on the table.

"Food," she declared. "As ordered."

"Mmm. Stew. Bread. Pickles. And wine!" Killian held up the bottle with a smile.

Always happy. How did he do it?

I joined him and Hannah to eat and listen.

Hannah carried the first part of the conversation.

"So we're currently in a Knight-managed safe house. This manor is meant to withstand attack. The windows all have bars. The walls are stone. The roof is slate tile. Meaning pretty much impervious to dragon fire. It's also situated on hallowed ground. The blessing seems to do a decent job of repelling some of the Grimm Effect."

"So I won't turn back into a beast?" I really didn't want to go through that again.

"Active curses aren't affected, but things like bespelled rats, giggling gingerbread men, or fiddling cats don't seem to be able to make their way onto the grounds or into the house. You should be safe in this room, but just in case, Gerome and I will take turns bedding down in front of your door."

"Inside or outside?" Killian clarified.

"Inside. The doors are too thick for us to break down quickly."

"Guess no hanky-panky tonight, then," he said with a long-suffering sigh.

I jabbed him with my elbow. "Your mom isn't here. No need to pretend."

"Who says I'm pretending?" he quipped. "Crazy idea, but have you thought about how our marriage could be beneficial?"

"In what respect?" I asked, rather than laughing in his face.

"Because if we stay a couple, then that would mean no more women and loose shoes for me and no beasts for you."

"Assuming the curse accepts our fake marriage. Also, you seem to have forgotten what happened to me last night."

"You're back to normal now," he pointed out.

"Now being the key word. I might change back, again." I had a feeling we'd find out at dusk. Not all versions of Beauty and the Beast were the twenty-four-seven kind. I'd seen some that furred out by day, others that fanged out at night. No one could predict or understand why the beast mode affected some people differently. I was also the first female version, so who knew what I should expect?

"If it helps, I always wanted a cat. We can't have one in the castle. Mother is allergic."

I blinked at him then looked at Hannah to mutter, "Did he just call me a kitty?"

"Well, you do have claws," she replied dead-pan, reaching for some more bread.

"This marriage thing..." I waved my own chunk of gluten as I tried to express myself without completely shoving my foot in my mouth. "Let's say I agreed. Won't your mother expect babies?"

"Yes."

"Kind of hard without sex." I tried and failed to hold in a blush as I spoke bluntly.

"Who says we wouldn't have sex?"

I choked on my bite of bread, and Hannah gave me a vigorous pounding while Killian handed me my wine glass for a big gulp. As if a sip would be enough. I chugged, refilled my glass, and drank some more before wheezing, "You're talking about making this a real marriage."

"What other kind would it be?" he replied, looking innocent but for the spark of humor in his eyes.

"I assumed you meant in name only, not that you wanted the whole shebang."

"Okay, then to make it clear, I propose we make this a real marriage, which means googly eyes as we stare at each other, hand holding, copious lovemaking that might result in kids, snuggling in bed and all."

My heart just about stopped. "Uh…" Yeah, I didn't have a reply, mostly because my mind suddenly flashed to what he proposed, and my pulse started pounding.

Hannah rose abruptly. "I'm going to check on Gerome. Be right back." Hannah suddenly bolted, and I wanted to follow, yet at the same time, I wanted to hear more.

"Why me? We barely know each other."

"I wouldn't say that. I know you're smart. Brave. Beautiful." He ticked off compliments, and I drank more wine because, quite honestly, it was that or slink under the table. He listed way more positive things about me than I could have named.

At the end of his spiel, I blurted out, "But what about love?"

Killian leaned back in his seat and regarded me. "My parents had their marriage arranged, and I will be honest, they didn't love each other. Not at first, but they did have great respect and affection that turned into love. We're already at the respect part, and if you're worried about a spark, I assure you, you get my motor running." He winked.

I tingled, and my mouth went dry. "You say that now, but what if you meet someone and fall in love while married to me?"

"Won't happen."

"You can't know that."

He drummed his fingers on the table. "Actually, I can. If you're worried I'd cheat or ditch you, don't. I am not that kind of man. What say you, wifey poo? Shall we give this marriage a real go?"

He wanted an answer now? "Can I think about it?"

"Of course. On one condition."

"What condition?" I asked suspiciously.

"I want us to share a kiss so I can prove we have chemistry."

I already knew we did. "We already smooched at our wedding."

"That wasn't a real kiss, and you know it."

He had a point. I'd been so nervous at the time. Still, what he asked... I hesitated, not because I didn't want to kiss the prince but because I wanted to. I liked him, and I knew from past experience, that didn't end well. "I don't think it's a good idea."

"You worry I'll become a beast."

I nodded.

"Then we'll be able to commiserate."

"This isn't a joke. Being a beast will impact your life. Especially if you turned into the twenty-four-hour version."

"Would that be so bad? It would get me out of silly political theater."

"Your mom would murder me."

"No, she'd have someone else do it. She hates getting her hands dirty."

I pursed my lips. "Is this situation a joke to you?"

"No. This is one of the more serious things I've contemplated." His expression matched his tone.

"Contemplated?" I snorted. "We got married like not even two days ago."

"Two very interesting days," he countered. "With you, there is no pretense. You don't treat me like royalty. You call me out when I'm being blasé. You aren't afraid to speak up for yourself, which will be necessary with my mother. She can be a tad overbearing."

"Way to sell the marriage idea," my dry reply.

"I have every faith you can handle her."

"You're talking about me leaving my life, and my job, behind."

"That would be unavoidable, but in good news, the castle does have a library with room to move your books, and you'd be able to purchase as many more as you like. Once we replace the jet, you could visit or have your friends over anytime you desired. As for your employment, you would be my princess, eventually queen, with more than enough tasks to keep you busy."

I grimaced. "Yeah, that's not a selling point." What I didn't add was he did have me intrigued. I'd given up on the idea of marriage and having a family. Could we make this work? I did enjoy his company, despite his always-cheerful attitude. "What would you get out of it, other than a lack of shoes being dropped every time you turn around?"

"A partner I can respect. A person I can count on."

"I know nothing of royal protocol."

"Another selling point if you ask me. I don't want or need someone flighty by my side, nor someone raised to be pampered and snobby."

"Ah, so you like me because I'm a commoner."

"You are far from common, wifey poo." His smile melted my insides but I held strong.

I rolled my eyes. "Calling me that isn't the way to convince me."

"What will?"

I almost said him loving me, which, again, would be too much to expect this soon. I couldn't even say I loved him, but I did like him, more than expected.

"I'll think about it." I held up a finger. "But no kissing, yet. Let's see first how we do together before I possibly turn you into a beast."

He nodded. "My wife wants to be wooed. Understandable."

"Woo? What?"

"I shall highlight my many awesome attributes while doing my best to show you how compatible we would be together."

"Show me how?" A suspicious lilt to my query.

He smiled. A panty-wetting version as he purred, "You'll see. Now, shall we explore the manor? I don't know about you, but I like to know where the exits are, as well as the pantry."

"Plotting how you're going to sneak in for a midnight snack."

"Afternoon, actually, and probably early evening."

I shook my head. "Good thing you're a prince and

not a Hansel. That witch would have fattened you up for cooking in no time."

"I wonder if her food was any good," he mused aloud. He stood from the table and held out his arm. I slid my hand into the crook of it, a tingle going through me at the simple touch. "Shall we?"

"Lead the way. *Husband.*"

Weird how it sounded so right.

9

We explored the manor, shadowed by Gerome, who picked us up the moment we left the bedroom. The place had many empty spaces, the doors wide open showing off their contents. Bedrooms in the east wing, the mattresses bare of sheets, a thin layer of dust on the furniture. The west wing had been converted into storage for weapons, canned goods, clothing, and more.

I eyed the accumulation of stuff and murmured, "It's like a stockpile for the apocalypse."

"Because it is. We've done the same in Corsica. Mother has concerns that if the Grimm Effect were to increase its infection rate, supply chains would be disrupted."

"Which is looking more and more likely these days," I murmured in reply.

"Good thing we're doing something about it."

I wish I had his confidence.

We finished our tour in the training room. While Gerome skulked in a corner, Killian headed for the rack of weapons, pulling a long sword. "Nice blade," he remarked.

"Do you know how to use it?" I asked.

"I'm very adept with my sword," he said with a wink.

Yeah, we won't discuss what that did to my nether regions.

"I'm more of a throwing-dagger kind of girl," my reply.

"Show me." He pointed to an array of knives hung on a magnetic board.

"If you insist. Do you have an apple to put on your head?" I quipped, grabbing a dagger and feeling its weight before swapping it for another with a nicer balance.

"Not until I see you throw first," he riposted with a chuckle.

"Where's the trust, husband?" It got easier every time I said it.

"It's said death is quicker than divorce."

"Probably less messy too." My humor ran a little darker than his.

He still laughed. "All right, wifey poo, let's see what you've got."

Him and his wifey-poo. The most ridiculous thing he could call me.

I whirled and flung the blade, aiming it about two feet off his left side. To his credit, he didn't flinch, but he did whistle as I hit the target dummy behind him in the chest.

"Nice throw. Can you do that consistently?"

I showed him. Grabbing and flinging knives, one after another in rapid succession, all but one sticking in the target circle. It nicked the handle of another and plinked to the ground.

He whistled. "Impressive. Now the next question, how are you in hand-to-hand situations?"

"Want to find out?" I beckoned with my fingers.

"Ooh, a challenge. How can I resist?" he stated, heading for the knife wall, while I grabbed my favorite from the dummy.

"I get the impression you're the type who only needs a single dare and not a triple dog dare."

"Right you are."

"Must have driven your mom nuts."

He cast me a grin over his shoulder. "Right again. You should have heard her ranting when I broke my leg jumping from the barn roof."

"Why would you do that?"

"Well for one, Daryl dared me, and second, Suzie McInnis was watching. The hay bale should have broken my fall."

"What went wrong?"

"I bounced off it into the tractor."

I winced. "Ouch."

"Yup. But in better news, Suzie was so impressed by my bravery, she shared her lunch with me for a month."

I couldn't help my laughter. "You and food."

"You know, they say the way to a man's heart is through his stomach."

"Is this a bad time to mention I'm a terrible cook?"

"Good thing I can afford a chef."

"Glad to hear it. I'd never be able to afford your grocery bills on my salary."

"Which is why it's good to know how to farm. Nothing better than growing and eating something you nurtured. Ready?" He took up a stance opposite me, but before we could begin sparring, Gerome cleared his throat.

"Not without blade guards you aren't."

The gruff man insisted we wrap the daggers in the foam sheaths meant for practice bouts. With the sharp edges hidden, we began our match. Small feints at first, but as Killian showed he knew how to move, I stepped up my game. Spinning and slashing, ducking and sliding under his guard to tap him above the waist.

"Bye-bye, kidney," I sang.

"Nice move." He complimented, unlike some male agents who got bent out of shape when I bested them. My shooting might be mediocre and swords too tiring, but daggers? I loved them almost as much as books.

As we continued to parry, he talked. "How come I've never seen you with a knife?"

"Because people tend to freak when they see sharp weapons. So either I have my taser on me, which is better for subduing, or I've got it tucked out of sight."

"Have you ever had to use it in the course of your work?" He avoided my slash by raising his arm to block.

"The dagger, no, but I have zapped a few belligerent grimphers. They're not always appreciative of us getting them out of a bind."

"I heard your office recently solved a big serial killer case."

"Yeah, the media called it Hood and the Huntsman." I feinted to my left, only to drop low and slash his leg to the right. "Artery gone," I chirped then continued as if I hadn't just killed him. "The killer had us running circles with all kinds of false leads and a string of bodies, but in the end, we took him down. And by we, I mean Blanche and her boyfriend."

"Sounds dangerous."

"I'm a Fairytale agent. It's part of the job."

"Speaking of danger, what of the beasts you encounter? Do you often have to put them in their place?"

"It's been a while since I've had to grab one by the balls and remind it that being an animal doesn't give them the right to act like one with me."

His hands dropped to his groin. "Ow."

"Yes ow, and very effective. It's—"

Crash. The skylight overhead shattered, and despite the bars over it to prevent intrusion, birds slid through the gaps between the slats. Ravens, dozens of them, their wings fluttering rapidly enough the noise made it almost impossible to hear Killian's shout.

"Get out of here."

"You get out," I hollered as I took aim and threw my knife.

One bird down. I ran for the dummy with the blades I'd tossed earlier and began grabbing and throwing. Hit a bird, and it went down. Another toss impaled the next. But more winged for me while ignoring Killian and Gerome, and this despite the fact both men slashed with their swords, shearing wings and sending the birds plummeting.

Guess the ravens had come for me.

And kept coming even when I ran out of knives. I

put my arms over my head to cover my face as wings beat at me and beaks pecked at the cotton covering my arms.

However, that pain paled to that of the crackling as the beast suddenly emerged from my skin.

Dusk had arrived, and when the transformation finished, I didn't need a knife.

My claw-tipped hands grabbed and ripped. I roared. I stomped.

By the time the last bird hit the ground, I was a mess, my fur slick with gore and even feathers.

And what did my husband say? "Good, kitty."

10

I stared in horror at my bloody claws. Murdering paws. Even worse, I'd exulted while in the midst of battle.

I'm a monster.

Not according to the prince. "Now, now, don't you dare get mopey on me. You were incredible."

"I killed them with my bare hands," I whispered, my voice the gruffer version of itself.

"You protected yourself."

How to explain that, while it began that way, I'd felt a rush as I fought and won.

Gerome barked, "Out of this room in case there's more coming." As we hustled into the main hall, Gerome bellowed, "Hannah!"

She must have been nearby because she came skidding into view. Her eyes widened at the sight of me, and she muttered, "Holy shit. What the fuck happened?"

"Birds. Training room. Broke through the window."

Clive arrived to hear the latter and uttered, "Impossible. The manor is..." His words trailed off and his eyes widened at the sight of me. "Where did this beast come from?"

"Hey, Clive. Don't panic. It's me, Belle." I waved a furry paw.

"You were saying?" Killian redirected Clive's attention.

"Uh, I was saying the manor is protected from incursion."

"Is it? Or has it simply never been tested?" Killian spoke more seriously than I was used to hearing.

Clive's mouth opened and shut before he shook his head. "Perhaps we assumed wrong."

"I need somewhere safe to bring my wife that she might clean herself up. Preferably a bathroom with no window." Killian made the demand, and Clive started to shake his head before grimacing.

"Only one room with running water and no windows. But it's in the basement."

"Perfect," Killian exclaimed.

Clive's lips pursed. "I should warn you, it's not exactly nice."

"We don't need nice. We need safe. Show us." Killian didn't ask, he ordered, and Clive led the way.

In shock, I could do nothing but numbly follow, big hairy feet plodding, the socks I'd been wearing stretched to their new size. Clothes, too. Guess the beast thing would be a recurring part of my life now. I'd not even realized the day had gotten so late. I wonder how the bird fight would have ended had I not shifted. Possibly with me lacking eyes. I'd heard ravens liked to pluck them.

The stairs down from the main level to the basement were made of stone, worn in the middle to form a dip on each step. The lighting proved harsh, single bulbs hung on a wire at intervals in a space that would have been pitch-black without since, as promised, the basement lacked windows.

The chamber Clive led us to turned out to be a bathroom, one not used in a long time judging by the brown ring inside the toilet and the dust and cobwebs stretched across the chipped, claw foot tub. No shower, though.

"Thank you. Leave us alone." Killian waved his hand. Clive left, but Gerome and Hannah stood just within the door, which led to my husband snapping, "A bit of privacy please."

"We'll be in the hall." Hannah grabbed Gerome and yanked him out with her.

"Let's get these clothes off you," Killian murmured, which was when I finally reacted, slapping his hand.

"I can undress myself. Turn around." I didn't want him seeing me naked for the first time like this. My beast shape still had boobs, covered in hair, no tail at least, but a furry ass and a coochie that would have cost me a fortune if I'd gone to an esthetician for a Brazilian.

The prince gave me his back, and I undressed with shaking hands, er, paws. My clothes hit the floor, and I approached the tub and turned on both faucets. Rusty brown water gushed out, mixing with the dust before swirling down the drain. The water remained cold, despite me having opened both taps. I girded myself for the chill as I stepped into the tub, my toes curling at the freezing water. No showerhead meant I had to crouch, rinsing my hands under the stream then splashing it on my face. I kept my eyes closed to ignore the dirty pink scuzz that sluiced from my fur.

I quickly went numb, not just in body but spirit. Odd how the dragon attacks hadn't traumatized me, but embracing my beast side, using it to kill, did. Would the daily flip into monster mode change me? I'd seen it happen before.

"How's it going?" Killian asked.

"Fine." A soft reply.

"You did nothing wrong."

"Tell that to my shaking hands," I replied with a tremor in my voice.

"You fought to save yourself."

"It's not the fight so much as the rush I got." The truth slipped out because that was probably the most horrifying part. I'd reveled in prevailing. Found joy in killing the ravens.

"When in life-or-death situations, that kind of adrenaline is normal. When it's you against adversity, it's okay to feel good about winning."

"Then why do I feel so bad?" I whispered.

I never heard him move, but suddenly he was in the tub with me, his arms wrapping me from behind. "Because you're a good person."

I snorted. "Am I?"

"Yes." He squeezed me. "A bad person wouldn't give a damn about what they did. Wouldn't question their own morality."

"I'm afraid," I admitted.

"That's okay too. You're dealing with a sudden change. The curse is actively targeting you. You'd be a fool to be blasé about it."

"Maybe this trip was a bad idea."

"Say the word and I'll whisk you away."

I craned to see him. "You'd do that?"

"Yes. In a heartbeat."

"Why does it feel like there's a but?"

"How long before you regret giving up? Before you take a look at our evolving world and the increasing curses and wish you'd persevered?"

"The curse doesn't want me looking for answers."

"Isn't that all the more reason to keep going? It's frightened of you. Why else would it be trying so hard?"

"Scared of me?" I couldn't help a rough chuckle. "I don't even know what I'm looking for, and even if I find something, what if I can't figure out how to stop it?"

"Then at least we'll have tried."

We. He liked to use that word. Acted as if we were already a couple. "You know, it would be simpler and safer for you to walk away."

"I thought we'd already determined I can't say no to a challenge."

"Exactly. I'm putting you in danger with my crazy idea."

"It's not crazy to want to act," his soft reply.

"How about at the very least I shouldn't be dragging others along with me."

"You're not dragging me, wifey-poo. I'm as determined as you to see this through."

"Hannah and Gerome didn't exactly have a choice," my low mutter.

"Do you really think either of them would walk away?"

"Like fuck!" Hannah yelled from the hall, showing she listened.

I ducked my head into my bent knees. "It feels so overwhelming." What seemed like such a novel and simple idea, find the source of the Grimm Effect, had snowballed into so much more.

"You're not alone." He hugged me tight. "Now, let's get you out of this tub and dried off before you start shaking wildly and flinging water everywhere."

"I'm not a dog," my tart reply.

"Nope, you're a sexy kitty. *Rawr*." He mock-roared as he stood, pulling me up with him. "Hannah, did Clive fetch some towels?"

"Bringing them in," she stated. "And don't worry Belle, I won't peek. I've no interest in seeing your naked kitty."

In short order, Killian had me wrapped in a towel. Only then did I turn to face him and saw his soaked clothing, a result of him comforting me. "You're wet too."

"Yup." He stripped the shirt, and I got a peek at my husband's chest. Lean and muscled. Tanned as well. I could do way worse. But good looks weren't the only thing I wanted in a marriage.

He toweled his upper body off then tossed me a

grin as he said, "Let me say right now, it's the cold water's fault."

I didn't grasp what he meant until he grabbed his pants and pulled them down.

A proper person would have turned away to give him privacy. I gaped. I mean, for a guy blaming cold water for his size, he still seemed rather impressive.

And it got bigger the longer I stared.

When it pointed in my direction, I turned my head, and what do you know, a beast could blush.

"Told you we had chemistry," his soft murmur.

"Speak for yourself." Couldn't have said why I lied.

He chuckled. "You seem to forget how often you blush."

Hold on, he'd noticed?

Dammit.

"I'm decent."

Not really. He wore a towel sarong-style around his waist, leaving his chest bare.

And tempting.

Good thing I wasn't myself or I might have mauled him.

I still might.

I did the only thing I could think of to distract him. "I'm hungry. Think we can scrounge some food?"

His expression turned even more bright. "Dinner time! Hell yeah."

Only they wouldn't allow me upstairs to eat. Every room had a window. Barred, but now that we'd had one attack, everyone feared another.

It led to me grumbling to Hannah, "You're supposed to be guarding the prince, not me."

"You're now royalty, too, and the one who is being targeted, so suck it up, princess."

I grimaced in her direction. We sat in another basement room, quickly swept clean by Killian, while Gerome brought down a table and chairs for us to use. Me? I got relegated to sitting and compiling a report because, despite my having fat furry fingers, apparently I still remained the most adept with a computer.

The bureau would want to hear about the incidents. The dragons. The ravens. Never mind the fact we'd embarked on an unsanctioned mission. Agents and Knights had been involved in attacks. A crown prince imperiled. Add in the fact that I now found myself in a twisted version of my Beauty and the Beast curse, there was much to report.

By the time I finished and ran a spell checker for my chunky finger mistakes, a feast had been cobbled together, as well as clothing and weapons. A set of daggers on a cross-body harness for me, plus an ankle strap, a sword, and another dagger for Killian.

We dined on crusty bread, slabs of roast beef, horseradish, pickles—which Killian couldn't get enough of—and water. No wine, not with everyone wanting a clear head for the night ahead, a time when the curse seemed to thrive.

For bedtime, Gerome and Clive dragged down some mattresses and bedding. Two sets to be exact. Hannah took one, as she and Gerome would be taking turns on guard. The larger one was for me to share with the prince. For first watch, Gerome stood guard outside the chamber, while Clive kept an eye and ear open on the main floor. Not a large group if we came under concentrated attack, however, a call had been put out to bring more Knights. If they could get away from their current missions.

Apparently, in the last few hours, things had gone haywire. Inanimate objects coming to life and chasing their owners. A broom actually beat the woman who usually wielded it. We had a pied piper stealing children in Padstow and a myriad of other mischievous characters running agents and Knights ragged. A bakery in London had an entire batch of gingerbread men suddenly come to life to cause havoc.

It didn't take a genius to realize the curse did its best to prevent reinforcements. I lay on the mattress facing the wall, and Killian tucked in behind me. Despite being new to this kind of intimacy, I enjoyed the snuggling.

The proximity reminded me of our earlier conversation. His suggestion we remain married. I could see the benefits but also the problems. For one, I had no interest in being a princess or eventually a queen. Although the library he'd mentioned did tempt.

What about love, though? I liked the prince, no denying that, but like wasn't love. Not yet, at any rate. That might change, however. The man might be a joker, yet at the same time, he had a sweet side. A caring side. Look at how he'd taken care of me when I'd been in shock. How he snuggled me now despite my monster shape.

Would being his wife be so bad?

What if I ruined him with a kiss? He might be nonchalant about the curse turning him into a beast. However, the reality might hit him harder than he realized.

If the curse infected him. With me already being furry, would it still try and change him too? I wish I had a way of knowing for sure.

I fell asleep and had vivid dreams, of me, in beast form, chasing Killian through the woods. I eventually caught him and ate him but not in a way he complained about. On the contrary, he groaned in pleasure and... Let's just say we did things people shouldn't, especially when one wasn't herself.

I woke to find myself still wrapped in Killian's arms.

It would be nice to have this every night. At the same time, if we halted the Grimm Effect, he'd have no reason to stay married to me, a thought that saddened and sobered. It appeared I might already be losing my heart.

11

Morning came, and so did my skin. I patted my face to ensure the smoothness. No beard or mustache. A peek in my undies showed a normal-sized bush. For now. I had no doubt, by nightfall, that would change. I'd have to make the most of the day.

Knowing the clock ticked before my next shift had me eager to head out, a departure that would have been easier if something hadn't crushed the cars overnight.

Like, literally.

After we all showered and had breakfast, we stood outside looking at the squashed vehicles in the driveway. The confiscated car from the agents the day before and Clive's MINI Cooper. The windows had shattered from whatever had dented the roof.

"Well, that's not going to be a fast fix," Clive drawled.

"We're stuck." I jutted my lower lip in a pout.

Clive guffawed. "Bah, that's not my only means of transportation. How do you feel about travelling old school?"

By that, he meant horses and a carriage, the kind with big hoop wheels and enclosed seating, except for the driver who sat outside on a bench at the front.

"Um..." I stared because, quite honestly, I'd never seen the likes in real life before.

"Don't you worry. Bessy and Bertha are solid gals, aren't you?" Clive stroked the muzzles of the horses.

"Won't a carriage take longer?" I remained all too aware the clock ticked before my next beastly change.

"Once we get to Padstow, we'll rent a car," Hannah reassured.

At her claim, Clive shook his head. "Padstow's got a barricade up and ain't allowing outsiders anywhere close to town. We ain't the only ones with trouble last night. Word is the whole town's shut tight while they clean up the mess. Something about foxes and hens, cookie crumbles, and dragon shit."

Yikes. I hoped I'd not been the cause for the chaos overnight.

"If Padstow is out, then I guess we'll be travelling a little farther before we swap horsies for a car." Hannah glanced at Gerome. "You handling the horses or riding shotgun?"

"I've seen how you drive," Gerome grumbled as he clambered onto the seat.

Hannah stepped onto a ledge at the back and looped her arm through a rail. Her other hand gripped a rifle.

The prince opened the door to the carriage and flipped out a little step before offering me a hand. "After you, wifey poo."

I rolled my eyes. "That is a ridiculous nickname."

"And here I'm rather fond of it."

"Very well, hubby dubby." Probably the lamest comeback in the history of comebacks. I placed my hand in his and climbed inside the carriage. It had worn leather seats that faced each other, meaning I had no choice but to look at Killian.

He lounged across from me, looking relaxed as we lurched into motion. It proved to be bumpier than expected, and I slid around until he grabbed hold of me and dragged me into his lap.

"What are you doing?" I squeaked.

"Preventing a concussion."

I'd like to claim he exaggerated, but... I kind of liked my new spot. His arms wrapped around me, and his face nuzzled my hair, but it was the burgeoning erection under my bottom that heated my cheeks.

"So once we get to the hamlet Ashbrittle, we'll

have to be observant," I stated breathily to try and distract myself.

"Mmm-hmm."

"Given Ashbrittle appears to have experienced the earliest cases, chances are the source is nearby."

"But most likely hidden since no one's ever seen or mentioned anything."

"Or they didn't know what they found. We'll have to question the village folk."

"And what shall we ask?"

That was a stumbling point. "I don't know," I had to admit.

"We should have brought a drone."

"What for?"

"An aerial view might have shown us any structures that don't appear on a map. Perhaps some terrain anomalies."

"Maybe we'll find one in the town when we stop to rent a car."

He didn't reply, but he did kiss my nape, sending a shiver down my spine. When he did speak, it was to softly murmur, "Have you given thought to my suggestion?"

I could have played dumb. Instead, I half turned in his lap. "You still want to stay married to me after all that's happened?"

"As if a few dragons, ravens, and car-crushing monsters would change my mind." His lips held a smile.

"And the fact I'm hairy half the day?"

"Would you feel better if I stopped shaving? We could be hairy in solidarity."

"Hardly the same."

"You haven't seen the facial hair I can grow," he boasted.

"You're really determined."

"I am, especially when it's something I believe in."

"How can you be so sure we'd work? We haven't even properly kissed."

"Only because you wanted to wait."

It wasn't that I wanted to wait. I wanted to kiss him. So much. But what if... What if I cursed him?

He read my mind and whispered, "I'm willing to take that chance."

Before I could change my mind, I pressed my mouth to his. Just a touch.

Nothing happened, unless the tingling that started between my legs counted.

"That's not a kiss, wifey poo," he complained when I pulled away.

"I don't have much experience," I had to admit. Usually, by this point, I was fending off claw and fangs.

"Then let me show you how it's done." His mouth slanted over mine, claiming, branding me with passion. My breath hitched at the sensations that raced through me. Excitement, desire, urgency.

I wanted more. Especially since he remained human. That had never happened before. Usually by now, there was roaring and hair pulling, and blame. So much blame.

Our teeth clashed as I kissed him back, clumsy but eager. His hands helped to turn me so I sat straddling him, all the better to mesh our mouths.

But our lips weren't the only things having fun. His hands roamed me. Sliding up my back, squeezing my bum. I kneaded his shoulders and stroked his arms, reveling in the fact I could touch him. My pussy pressed against his groin, his erection a hard bulge that felt good when I rocked just right.

I could have done this all day, but he whispered, "Turn around so your back is tucked to my chest."

I wasn't questioning the man who had me floating. I flipped as asked and figured out the why really quick as his hand slid into my pants. I gasped when he touched me. It felt wondrous and strange. Previously, I'd been the only one to lay fingers on that intimate part of me. I liked it better when he did it. The tip of his finger circled my clit, parted my nether lips, teased me to the point I writhed on his lap.

He sat me on the bench and knelt before me, tugging down my pants, and I was too lost in the pleasure to care he could see me. He kept touching me. Stroking me. Making me claw at the leather seats at the pleasure.

When he blew hotly on me, I came off the seat for a second as I clenched in bliss.

He pinned my thighs and did it again. I shuddered as I came, a tiny orgasm that squeezed my eyes tight and my pussy even tighter.

But he wasn't done.

His lips touched me next, and his tongue, and... oh.

Oh.

He stroked me with his mouth, made me feel things I'd never imagined. Brought a coiling intensity to my body that had me striving for a peak I'd never even come close to reaching before.

I came. Not a tiny little orgasm that barely satisfied. I finally grasped what the books meant when they claimed to see stars. I floated, undulated, clenched, and expanded. The pleasure was unlike anything, and as I lay there limply, basking in the afterglow, I could only murmur, "Wow."

"That's nothing, dear wife. The pleasure has only just begun."

"Really?" It took effort to open my heavy eyes, and

no surprise, he knelt between my legs with a pleased grin.

A smile I ruined when the carriage abruptly halted and I slammed into Killian's face.

12

As the carriage suddenly halted, I scrabbled to pull up my pants. Got my coochie hidden—but could do nothing about my burning face—as the door opened and Hannah stuck her head in.

"We've got a problem," she announced.

"What kind?" asked Killian as he hopped out. Despite the urgency in Hannah's tone, he still half turned to offer me a hand and a smile.

I tried to not quiver as I recalled what that mouth had done.

Rather than reply, Hannah pointed. Lying directly across the road, a shoe. A giant shoe straight from the Victorian era, the kind with a leather exterior, a high top, laces, a zipper down the side, and empty eyelets.

I only knew of one rhyme that might apply.

"There was an old woman who lived in a shoe," I murmured.

"If that is the correct poem, then we should only be dealing with children and maybe their mother," Killian replied.

Guess we'd soon find out, as Gerome stomped to the giant shoe and hunched down to grab hold of the heel. I would have been impressed if he'd managed to move it, but grunting and heaving with all his might did nothing but make him sweat.

Instead of helping him, Hannah had her gun out and a wary expression. "I think you should move away from there, Gerome."

He glanced at her and might have grunted his usual reply if not for the arrow tipped with a suction cup that fired from an eyelet set higher up in the footwear. It stuck to his forehead and led to Gerome glaring upward.

"Stay here." Hannah approached the shoe to join her grumpy partner just as the zipper on the side opened and out poured a horde of knee-high youngsters, hooting and hollering, firing more plastic arrows but also slinging marbles.

The poor Knights, they didn't know how to react. On the one hand, they were being pelted, but on the other... these were children.

Even Killian appeared torn.

Me? I'd had my after-glow interrupted for this and was in no mood.

I planted my hands on my hips and in my best Hilda boss voice shouted, "Stop that at once."

The children paused and eyed me.

"That is not appropriate behavior," I chided. "Where's your mother?"

A ginger-haired tyke with a gap-toothed smile grinned as he said, "We tied her up when she wouldn't feed us."

Oh.

Not how the nursery rhyme went, but I could see why they'd acted, seeing as how the verse had something about whipping the children soundly.

"While I'm sure she deserved it for sending you to bed without dinner and punished on top of it, that doesn't mean you can accost people on the road." I gave no quarter. They didn't care.

"Says who?" huffed the ginger.

"Says me!" I snapped.

Their heads all cocked at the same time, in the same direction, and their expressions went glazed before they all nodded in synchronization and murmured, "Yes, papa curse."

A chill went through me, especially since they started staring at me. Remember that blank spooky scare from *Children of the Corn*? Even worse in person, especially since they leapt from the shoe and ran in my direction.

Bloody hell.

I would have bolted, but to where? Energetic children would easily catch me. So I braced myself, and they hit me in a swarm, tiny fists pummeling while they chanted, "Go away. Go away."

It didn't really hurt, but I was at a loss for what to do. I couldn't exactly slap them off.

Killian looked confused as well until Gerome shouted, "Beware the sky."

Now what?

A dark swarm approached, ravens, most likely, except for the much larger shape in their midst. A dragon. Probably the one that got away after the plane attack, back for round two.

The horses panicked and bolted, taking the carriage with them. The children fled next, screaming as they ran into their shoe house and tugged the zipper shut.

We had nowhere to hide.

But Killian didn't let that daunt him. He stood in front of me, a sword out, his expression grim. That's how I knew shit was serious.

Hannah hollered, "There's too many for us to fight."

The incoming flock was more than we'd dealt with

in the training room at the manor, and I was hours from beast mode. Look at me being disappointed I couldn't fur out at will.

How would we survive the coming battle? What would impede birds and a dragon?

The sunny sky made me wish for rain. And then I got the dumbest idea. "Rain, rain, go away, come again another day. Little Belle. Little Belle. Little Belle wants to play."

"What are you doing?" huffed Killian.

"Something new." That might not work, but I had to try. Since the sky remained blue, I went to my next song. "Rub-a-dub-dub, four people in a tub, and who do you think they'd be? A prince and his wife and two brave Knights, and all of them out to sea."

The ground remained dry, not a tub in sight, and the flock neared.

I tried one last song. "It's raining, it's pouring, Killian was snoring. He jumped from bed and bumped his head and couldn't get up in the morning."

Still nothing and the horde now darkened the sky overhead.

Killian cleared his throat. "Let's try one more. Together this time." He linked his hand with mine and started singing, "I hear thunder."

I knew this one and joined in.

"I hear thunder, I hear thunder.
   Hark, don't you? Hark, don't you?
   Pitter-patter raindrops,
   Pitter-patter raindrops.
   I'm wet through,
   So are you."

When we began to repeat the rhyme, to my surprise, Hannah joined in even as the cloud of wings began to drop, some of the birds arrowing for their dive. On the third verse, Gerome's deep baritone blended, and I might have wondered if we were insane but for the rumble overhead.

The encroaching darkness no longer came just from the birds and the dragon. Clouds had suddenly rolled in, and they looked angry.

So we kept singing, singing as the thunder actually began to boom. With it, lightning flashed, and a bolt of it hit the dragon's wing, sending it reeling. But the birds kept coming, the flutter of their wings almost drowning us out.

Until the rain came.

The downpour started hard and fast, a drenching torrent that sent the ravens scattering, Gerome too. He jogged off, spear in hand. Don't ask me where he pulled it from. I might have wondered why until I saw the shape huddled atop the shoe, hissing, the glow in its mouth showing a fire building.

The dragon was no match for Gerome, who flung his spear. The dragon took it through the throat. When it toppled, Gerome was already in motion, ready to finish it off. As for the birds, the rain scattered them, leaving us soaked, unharmed, and stranded by the road.

Killian hugged me to his side. "Quick thinking. How did you know it would work?"

"I didn't." But I'd remembered something I'd read, an opinion piece that had ruminated about how the Grimm Effect used magic to shape and even create events to suit storylines. So who was to say humans couldn't do the same? What if we could also wield that magic, in this case by using a rhyme to trigger it?

I'd thought the idea ridiculous when I read it, but with nothing to lose, for some reason, it popped into my head.

"I can't believe I just sang a kid's song instead of fighting," Hannah grumbled. "That said, do you know one to bring back the horses?"

I shook my head, and she sighed. "Then I guess we're walking."

Turned out, we didn't have to walk far. Just past the shoe, and over the hill, we found our carriage, the steeds grazing by the side of the road. In short order, we were off again and made it to a small hamlet, where a wad of cash bought us a Fiat.

If you've never seen one, it's tight. As in Gerome drove with his knees to his chest, the backseat had me sitting sideways to give Killian more leg room, and each bump felt as if our asses slammed off the ground. But just after lunch, we made it to Ashbrittle. Too late, apparently.

Despair filled me as I looked around and whispered, "It's gone."

Only ashes and ruins remained, as the hamlet had burned to the ground.

So much for finding any clues. We'd come for nothing, but even worse, we'd failed before we'd even had a chance.

I glanced at Killian. "Now is not the time for optimism. There's nothing left. No one to talk to. Nothing to search."

"If that were true, then why did the curse try so hard to turn us away?"

I opened my mouth to reply, only I had no answer. He made a good point, though. "The fire is meant to deter, to keep people from looking for something still here," I muttered. Something it didn't want us to see. "Where do we start searching?"

As if my query conjured it, a mist moved in, thick and moist, reducing our visibility to only a few paces around.

"That's a thick fog." Killian grabbed my hand. "Let's make sure we don't lose each other."

Good idea. Hannah and Gerome moved in close, weapons out and alert. This would be a good time for an ambush.

A slight breeze ruffled my hair and swirled the ash.

From the mist emerged creatures, the shapes recognizable—fox, chicken, wolf, bear, swan—all animals seen in the fairytales but with something odd about them. Their movements disjointed, their eyes a dull solid black.

It took Gerome muttering, "Those ain't alive," for me to exhale, "Zombies!"

"Not exactly." Hannah darted with her sword and

13

We tumbled out of the tiny car and wandered amongst the ruins of Ashbrittle, the houses that once stood reduced to rubble with only sections of the stone walls standing. Other structures, which must have been wood framed, had even less. A set of concrete stairs that went nowhere. A fireplace that jutted from ashes.

"How did we not know this happened?" I murmured. A fire this big and devastating, taking out an entire hamlet, should have made the news.

"Do you really have to ask?" Hannah retorted.

Not really. The curse could seemingly do whatever it wanted.

"Guess we came here for nothing." My shoulders slumped.

"Don't give up so easily, wifey poo."

sliced through a swan, decapitating it. At its death, the creature exploded into a puff of ash.

"Golems," I muttered. Creatures animated and shaped by magic. But how dangerous could these monsters of ash be? I got my answer a second later when a swan extended its neck to peck at Hannah's sword. She grumbled as it tried to yank it from her grip.

"Stupid, not-real bird." She gave it a boot before chopping its head. Poof. It exploded in a cloud of dust but that didn't daunt the rest.

The battle began. Killian and I stood back-to-back, me with my dagger, him with his sword while Gerome and Hannah chose to dart in and hack at the ash menagerie. They dissolved quickly and easily. However, for each one they eradicated, another took its place. And another, the dust quickly reforming to strike again.

Stab, slash, poof.

Again.

And again.

It led to me huffing, "How long can we keep doing this?"

"As long as it takes." Hannah's grim reply.

"It's trying to tire us out," Killian's prediction.

And once that happened, we'd be dead.

"We need to get back in the car and leave before we're overrun," I stated.

"Fuck giving up," Hannah snarled, slashing a bear into dust.

"In that case, we need to move past them," I replied as I stabbed, over and over, the sheep that came trotting for me.

"How do we choose a direction?" Killian stuck by my side.

"If we're still looking for the source of the curse, then we need to push past the spot with the most golems in our path."

"So straight ahead," Killian murmured.

Where the ash golems clustered thickest, we formed a square, each of us a corner that stabbed anything that came close as we pushed our way deeper into the thick fog.

"Beware the ground," Gerome suddenly shouted.

I halted in place and glanced over at the Knight. Gerome had sunk knee-deep in the ground, the pavement gone, transformed into a bog that sucked at the feet. Killian tugged me back a pace before it could grab hold of me too.

"Fucking hell," Gerome cursed. He tossed his sword to the pavement and grabbed at the solid ground, but his fingers couldn't get purchase, and he kept sinking.

Hannah slid a foot toward him while still slashing anything that came close. "Grab my leg as an anchor and pull yourself out," she advised. Gerome hooked his hand around her ankle, and she braced before grunting and taking a step back.

Killian and I guarded their effort. A chicken, whose head I'd cut off, ran around for a moment before collapsing into dust.

"Something big is coming," Killian warned.

And then the mist parted to reveal an ash dragon, or so I assumed by its dead gaze and gray pallor. It opened its mouth, and while I didn't see the glow of fire, I still shouted, "It's going to breathe."

Gerome heaved himself free and rolled to his feet. He and Hannah dashed left, while Killian, grabbing hold of my arm, pulled me right.

The dragon blew. It exhaled ash that billowed and coated us, stinging my eyes and causing me to choke. We ran away from the noxious cloud, coughing and unseeing. My heart pounded at the effort, and when Killian halted, I bent over to hack up a lung.

The grit in my mouth left my tongue pasty, and I spat on the ground as I wheezed. "Did we lose it?"

"Yeah. But we also lost Hannah and Gerome."

"That's not good." I straightened to look around, the area we found ourselves in still misty but not as thick, probably because of the trees. We'd stumbled into a forest.

"Think we can find them?" I asked.

"Not in this fog." Killian didn't sugarcoat. "However, I do see a path." He pointed to a worn dirt rut that led through the woods. "It has to go somewhere."

I opened my mouth to point out it went in the opposite direction we'd come from but instead said, "The golems didn't follow us."

Strange. Why would they have given up the chase?

As we walked, cautiously peering side to side, I couldn't help but mutter, "If it's trying to kill us, why send those ash golems?"

"I'm not sure I follow," Killian replied.

It took me a second to orate what had been bugging me. "They were too easy to dispatch."

"A good thing."

"If the curse really wanted to remove us, why not send something more substantial? Harder to finish off?"

"You mean like that dragon and birds?"

"It already knows Gerome is a master dragon killer. And we could have taken shelter in the shoe from the birds."

"I doubt those kids would have liked it." He paused. "You are right, though. Why not send wolves? Or something equally dangerous?"

"Because it wants us alive."

"If that were true, then why the attack on the plane?"

I chewed my lower lip. "I don't know. Just spitballing because something doesn't make sense. Why try so hard to get us to turn back, only to suddenly set us on a path?"

Killian halted to eye the rutted track then behind us, where the mist had crept in, obscuring the route back. "It's herding us."

Not the most auspicious announcement. "Do we keep going?"

"We came for answers," his reply.

"We have no idea if following this path will lead us to them."

"Do you see another choice?"

No. I didn't.

Killian grabbed my hand and squeezed it. "Whatever happens, we'll be together."

It reassured more than expected.

We continued on our way, treading softly in the quiet and dim forest. I kept angling my head left and right, convinced something watched. Followed. I waited for an ambush that didn't happen.

Our sudden emergence into a sunny clearing jarred. I halted, as did Killian. We took in the quaint cottage with its picket fence and blooming garden.

Vibrant and colorful after the gloom and gray of the forest.

My hair lifted, and my heart pounded. An almost electrical feeling emanated from the house and had me whispering, "I think we found it."

No need to say what. This was it. The reason we'd come.

And it was inside the cottage.

"Ready?" I whispered.

"Always, dear wife."

We entered the garden, the flagstone path swept clean. The chair outside the front door empty. The table by its side held a basket with knitting supplies, indicating someone lived here.

The door remained shut at our approach, the window in it providing no peek because of the floral curtain strung across.

I glanced at Killian and murmured, "Should we knock?"

"Is it locked?" he countered.

Before I could put my hand on the knob to check, the door opened.

In the doorway stood another golem, this one constructed of paper, a living papier-mâché of a person lacking eyes with a rip above its chin for a mouth. Parts of it appeared scorched, as if someone had set it on fire. I could understand why, given its creep factor.

"You made it," the figure stated, its voice a singular tone with no inflection.

"Made it where?" I asked.

"The place you've been looking for." It stretched its paper mouth, causing parts of it to crack as it performed a parody of a smile.

"Who owns this house?"

"Someone you've met. But she's tied up for the moment."

"Why were we brought here?" Would this construct even know?

"Because it is time for the plan to evolve."

"Evolve how?" Killian queried.

"Come inside if you want to find out." It stood to the side and waited for us to enter.

I glanced at Killian, who shrugged.

He left it up to me. I'd not come this far to chicken out now.

As I entered, I couldn't help but shiver and think we'd just walked into the belly of the beast.

14

THE LAIR OF EVIL LOOKED QUAINT. I MEAN there was no other word for it. The sunny interior showed off the eclectic arrangement of furniture, wooden, the kind with spindled legs and ornate corners. Rugs covered the wood-plank floor. A floral wallpaper brought color to the space. The kitchen appeared from the nineteen fifties, the white cabinets still sporting big chrome knobs. The appliances the avocado green that used to be so popular.

I saw no sign of the owner. The golem strode into the living room area, which held a faded pink velvet couch and a plaid recliner. The small fireplace displayed logs ready for lighting. Lace doilies abounded, and a large, knitted blanket sat folded on a footstool.

"When can we speak to the owner of the house?" It felt odd talking to a magical construct.

"Why would you want to do that?"

"Because we have questions."

"About the Grimm Effect." The golem stood in front of the window, the glow of the sun around its edges making it hard to look at.

"Do you know anything about it?" Killian asked, sitting casually on the couch as if this were a social call.

"I know everything about it since I'm the one who set it loose."

I blinked. "You did?"

"You sound surprised." The golem kept speaking in that dull monotone. "I blame this vessel. It isn't as useful as I'd hoped."

I sat down hard beside Killian. "What are you?"

"Some would call me alien. But I am much more than that."

"Do you have a name?" I numbly asked, still caught on the alien part of its statement.

"I am Methuselah."

"Why does that sound familiar?" I muttered.

Killian knew the answer. "Isn't that a star?"

"Your astronomers call anything that glows in space a star," the thing scoffed. "I am the destroyer of worlds."

As the words fell into the silence left behind, I

couldn't help myself. "How is a paper puppet a destroyer? I mean look at you. You're scorched. You don't even have a face."

The slash of a mouth definitely crackled down at the corners. "Do not mock me. I am a force to be feared."

"Not right now you aren't." I really couldn't seem to stop running my mouth.

"It is not the container that counts but the spirit within."

"So you're a ghost?" I asked to clarify.

"Hardly. I am a god."

"Of puppets." Killian's turn to mock.

"And this is why I must upgrade this body," it grumbled.

"You know, you could try some paint. Give yourself some eyes. Maybe a wig," Killian suggested.

"Like lipstick on a pig," I muttered.

"No need for artifice when I won't be residing much longer in this shell," the paper construct stated.

A disturbing statement, but rather than poke more about that topic, I switched to something it said earlier. "You didn't seem surprised to see us arrive on your doorstep."

"Because you were expected."

"You wanted us to come here?"

"Are all humans this slow to comprehend?" No disdain in the statement but the intent was there.

"Just trying to understand why you were trying to kill us if you wanted us to find you."

"I wanted to ensure your worthiness."

"For what?" I couldn't help the suspicious note.

"Did you not hear when I said I needed to upgrade my container?"

A chill went through me. "You can't have my body."

"Why would I want yours?" I'd have sworn it tried to sneer. "The females on this world are the weaker of the species. Not to mention, you have no rank." Its head swiveled to Killian. "But a future king... That will suit me quite well."

"Oh hell no," I blurted out. "You can't have my husband either."

The thing cocked its head. "As if you have a choice."

"There's always a choice," I growled before lunging at it, dagger out. I stabbed it in the heart. The knife went through the rigid paper. I yanked it free to see a slit but no blood, just an odd green glow coming from within its shell.

The mâché man stood still. "Would you like to try that again? You can't kill me. Even if you destroyed the construct, my spirit would simply return to the stone."

"What stone?" I blurted out.

No surprise, the thing didn't reply. "There is much to do to prepare for the implantation of my spirit in the king's body."

"I'm a prince, not a king," muttered Killian.

"A minor inconvenience. Once the current monarch dies, you will ascend. From that position of power, I will be able to move about this world freely. As I conquer countries, they will fall under my control until there is one leader. Me."

I snorted. I couldn't help it. "You really think the world is going to bow down to you?"

"They will accede to my power," the golem stated, as if the people of Earth would just acquiesce on its say-so.

"What power?" Killian interjected. "Corsica is hardly an imposing country. Our main claim to fame is our exports. We barely have an army. We definitely don't have any nukes or weaponry that would intimidate anyone."

The thing clasped its hands. "You raise interesting points. However, in my research of your world leaders, most are feeble old men and women whose bodies couldn't handle the transference. You, however, are fit, not unattractive by this world's norms, and while your country is currently lacking in military strength, that will come when we align with a more powerful one."

"Align how?" I asked questions because I wanted to understand its plan. How else would we stop it? Never mind the fact I had no idea how we'd trap and vanquish this alien Methuselah. The more knowledge, the better. I still wondered what it meant by returning its spirit to the stone.

"I will align with a powerful nation via marriage. That is how most political alliances are formed."

"I'm already married," Killian pointed out.

"A minor inconvenience."

"You're going to kill me." I should have been scared, but instead, I spat in annoyance.

"Eventually. While not the ideal body, you would make an excellent backup should the transference fail with the king."

So I wouldn't die right away. Lovely. That might give me time to figure out a plan.

"For the transference to happen, you will need preparing." The golem addressed Killian.

"What kind of preparing?" I asked since Killian only glared.

"The taint of my magic is still upon him. It must be removed. Then there is the spirit, which also must go to make room for mine."

With each word, the knot in my stomach grew.

Killian finally reacted. "When you say my spirit has to go, what will happen to it?"

"It will be unbound from the flesh to become what you term a ghost, which will fade over time until the planet reabsorbs it for a rebirth."

"You can't do that," I exclaimed, fear finally hueing my tone.

"I will do whatever I like, and there is nothing anyone can do to stop me. Now, enough talk. You, female, will remain here in captivity in case things go awry with the king."

"And if I refuse?" I huffed.

"Willingly or by force. I do not care."

"I'm not doing anything you want," I spat. I'd resist every step of the way.

"Very well. By force it shall be." It said nothing else, and yet I heard a door open and shut, followed by a heavy tread.

To my surprise, Gerome entered the room.

My lips split into a smile. "Am I glad to see you. Shred its paper ass." I pointed to the golem.

Gerome swiveled his head to look but didn't pull a sword from his sheath.

The thing canted its head, and I swore it tried to smile. "He won't obey you. The Knight is enchanted and now serves me."

"Bullshit," I blurted out, even as my short-lived elation faded.

"The Knight did try and fight the compulsion but ultimately lost."

Judging by Gerome's blank gaze, true. It also meant we couldn't hope for rescue. Unless Hannah remained at large.

"Now, will you go docilely, or shall I have Gerome escort you forcefully?" A polite monotone request and I didn't like either option.

"Fuck you." Since Gerome blocked the path to the front door, I darted in the direction of a hall I saw branching off the living room. Most homes had two exits. Since the main one entered the kitchen, I might find one at the back. The first open door in the hall showed a bathroom with a small window. I went for the next door, hauling it open to see shelves with linen.

Dammit.

The door beside it ended up being a bedroom, the windows copious but narrow.

Only one door left.

I flung it open, hoping it would lead me outside or to a mudroom with access to the yard. Instead, I found myself in a study. Big wooden desk. Bookcases, with empty shelves probably because the books were stacked on a small side table. No exit, just more windows, but of more concern the woman sitting slumped on the floor, her gray hair wisping out of its bun, her frilly finery wrinkled.

"Fairy Godmother?" I murmured as I stepped inside.

Her head lifted, and I could barely see her eyes through the hair flopping in her face. I did hear her sigh.

"Oh, dear girl. You shouldn't have come."

"Too late for that." I whirled and slammed the door shut, as if that would stop the blank-faced Gerome doing the slow stride down the hall.

I leaned against the door and wondered what I could use to wedge it shut. I'd need a bit of a head start to escape from the window. Then I'd have to... do what exactly? I had no plan, not yet, but I figured if I could get to somewhere with a phone and put a call in to Her Majesty, she'd have some kind of armada to send to save her little prince. The bureau would likely send reinforcements too, especially once I explained I'd found the source of the Grimm Effect.

The desk chair had wheels, not ideal but I rammed it under the doorknob anyhow. With hands planted on my hips, I eyed the desk. Could I heave it over?

"You don't have to worry. Methuselah won't come in here."

I glanced at Godmother. "You obviously know about that thing."

"Oh yes. Although I didn't know it had an actual

name and personality until recently." Her lips turned down. "I made so many mistakes."

"You can tell me all about it once we get out of here."

I headed for the window and heaved at the window sash. It didn't budge.

"It won't open," she advised. "Methuselah made sure of that when he locked me in here."

I whirled. "Then I'll break it."

"Also not—"

The paperweight I tossed at the pane of glass bounced and almost landed heavily on my toe.

"—not possible," she finished saying. "Welcome to my prison."

"I'm not staying here," I muttered, more to encourage myself than reassure her.

"I said the same thing when Methuselah locked me in here after the ball." Her lips turned down. "He's strong, though, and tricky. He ensured I couldn't escape."

"What is that thing? It claimed to be an alien," I stated as I prowled the room looking for a way out.

"Because it is an alien."

I stumbled before whirling. "For real?"

"Yes. Although it doesn't have an actual body. It shot down from the sky in a tiny pebble-sized meteor. Not realizing what I'd found, I brought it inside and made the mistake of placing it on a book, and I started the mess that is the Grimm Effect."

My eyes widened. "Let me guess, the book was the Brothers Grimm fairytales."

She nodded. "Somehow, this alien rock absorbed those stories, but it wasn't until later that I realized it was making them come to life."

"It launched the curses."

"Yes."

"But why?" I blurted out. "Why is it doing this?"

"For more power. It calls itself the destroyer of worlds. From what I've gleaned, it ate a bunch of them, too many as it turned out, and it ran out of food, for lack of a better term. It was in a dormant state until it discovered Earth. Now that it's here, it's planning to rebuild its strength and use our planet as a base while it seeks out other planets with life it can devour."

"Damn." I couldn't think of anything else to say in that moment. It sounded so incredibly fictional.

"Damn indeed," she agreed with a sad nod.

"How come you never told anyone?" I accused. "We could have nipped this in the bud." Before it accumulated power.

"You have to realize, at first, I didn't understand what happened. The oddities started out small, and by the time I understood, it had spread."

"So why not tell anyone then?"

"I tried." Her lips turned down. "I invited a professor friend to see what I'd found. When he put his hand on the stone, he evaporated."

"Oh. Does that happen to anyone who touches it?"

She shrugged. "I don't know. No one else has dared. Nor has anyone else managed to get close other than me. The next two people I brought, which included a general in the military, never even saw the rock. Poor General Kilner got turned into a tree. He's still flourishing in my garden. As for the other, our representative in government, he became the first fiddler, and last I heard, he'd taken his life in a mental institution after they took away his fiddle."

"So you gave up?" I couldn't help an incredulous note.

"Of course not," she huffed. "I tried other things to diminish its effect."

It hit me in that moment. "You gave it more books."

"I gave it dry encyclopedias, which only made it smarter. I fed it kinder fairytales in the hopes of mitigating some of the darker tales it reenacted."

"I don't think it helped," I stated, thinking of the string of murders we'd recently handled, not to mention all the deaths that occurred from people caught up in the curse.

"I soon realized that and removed all books from my home, but it found ways to get more stories. As the fairy godmother, I found myself tugged away from home quite often. I'd try and do my task quickly, but a few times, I returned to find new books on the stack." She glanced over at the tower of books.

"Surely someone noticed a paper person walking around."

"That development was quite recent. I tried to get rid of it," she admitted softly.

"You're the reason it has scorch marks on its body."

"Yes. I tried to burn it. But its magic doused the flames, and it locked me in here."

"Why didn't it kill you?"

She shrugged. "I don't know. It doesn't think like a human."

"And yet it was talking about taking over a human body."

"Perhaps we could kill it once it's in true flesh," she mused aloud.

"We can't!" I shouted. At her dropped jaw, I added, "It's planning to take Killian's body. Prince Killian," I emphasized.

"Your husband," she murmured. Her lips gave a

sad lilt. "That poor prince. The irony being his and Cinder's actions actually rid the world of that curse. It's back in the book now where it belongs." She waved a hand and at my confused look explained. "When a story resolves in a certain manner, the magic is no longer able to use it. It counters its powers and returns it to the book."

"Which is good to know but doesn't help us because this is real life and not a story. At least not a story I've ever read."

"A pity because then we'd have a blueprint as to how to handle it." Godmother sighed.

Vrrrrm.

The engine noise drew me to the window, where a car idled in front of a small, detached garage.

As I watched, Methuselah, inside his paper puppet, emerged, strutting disjointedly, followed by Killian, and, rounding out their party, Gerome. My husband appeared to be sleepwalking, his expression blank.

He sat in the car beside the paper golem while Gerome took the wheel.

As they drove off, I exclaimed, "They're leaving." I whirled to ask, "Where are they going?"

"I don't know, child. I was not made privy to its plans."

I slumped to the floor. "We're so screwed."

"We are," Godmother agreed.

Despair crashed down on me, and I tucked my head to my knees, preparing to have a good sob when there was a tapping at the window.

My head whipped around, and I couldn't believe my eyes because someone stood outside.

"Hannah."

15

The Grimm Knight stood outside the window, peering in, hair wisping from her fat braid.

Elated that she'd found us, I rushed to put my hands on the glass and yelled, "Hannah, can you hear me?" I wasn't sure if the magic keeping us in also blocked sound.

"Yeah, I hear you."

"We're trapped and need help to escape."

"What's the situation inside? What am I facing?" Hannah kept her tone low and brisk.

"Well, the paper golem is gone—"

"The what?"

"Let's just say we found the source behind the curse. It's currently walking around in a person-sized paper puppet." A truly nut-sized version of what had occurred.

Hannah blinked before drawling slowly, "A paper puppet. Jeezus. Not what I expected."

"There's much to explain, but we can do that once you get us out of here."

Hannah peered past me and frowned. "Where's the prince?"

"He and Gerome left with the paper puppet."

"Gerome was here?" her sharp reply.

I nodded.

"Bloody hell. Guess that explains why I didn't find him," she muttered. "I assume there's a reason you haven't escaped via the window."

"I can't break the glass."

Her brow arched. "Did you use a pillow to hit it?"

Oddly, her sarcasm reassured. "Smartass. It's been magicked."

"Or you didn't put enough muscle into it with those tiny arms of yours. Stand back while I give it a shot," Hannah ordered with a wave of her hand.

Taking a few paces from the window brought me to Godmother's side. She stood, looking bedraggled in the fancy gown she'd worn to the ball what seemed like an eternity ago. As Hannah wound up for a swing, I murmured, "I never asked earlier, but given you're stuck, I assume Methuselah took your power to do miracles?"

Her nose wrinkled. "My gift is very narrow in scope. Transforming clothing, arranging transport, doing makeup, hair, those kinds of things."

"Surely you can do more. Cinder said you used magic to get her in the academy."

"Hardly magic. More like I pulled some strings with someone I knew. The agent who helped register her was a former Cinderella who escaped a prince who had a fetish for dressing as a dog and being walked. She had a soft spot for me, seeing as how I ensured her ballgown was etched in kittens and fringed in cat hair. Apparently, the prince was quite repulsed."

"Wait, if you know someone in the bureau, then that must mean they're aware of the alien rock."

"Unfortunately, no. After my failed attempts to find a way to nullify the stone, Methuselah cast a spell on me to prevent me from speaking of it."

"You're talking now."

"I assume he let the spell lapse. Now that he's gotten strong enough, he no longer cares who knows."

Wham. I glanced at the window to see Hannah staggering back from it, tree limb in hand. She gave it another go, running at the glass and swinging hard. The blow vibrated her head to toe and didn't even leave so much as a scratch.

"I'm going to try shooting it," she yelled.

Just in case it worked, we shifted out of the path the bullet might take.

Bam.

The glass didn't even quiver.

"Fuck this," Hannah hollered. "I'm coming through the front."

I glanced at Godmother. "Should I worry it left behind a surprise?"

She shrugged. "Who knows with that sadistic alien."

We couldn't hear anything from the rear of the house, not at first. Then there was cursing. Some banging. A high-pitched squeal. Then silence.

Click.

We eyed the door as the knob turned and opened. A bedraggled Hannah stood in the doorway, scowling. "Agatha. I should have known you were in the middle of this mess."

"Not by choice, I assure you."

"Your furniture attacked me," Hannah huffed.

"Oh, I hope you didn't have to murder my sofa. They don't make them like that anymore." Agatha wrung her hands.

Hannah's grimace deepened. "Afraid you'll have to go shopping."

"What yodeled?" I asked.

My question twisted Hannah's lips. "Me when the broom spanked me between the legs."

"Oh." I bit my lip so as to not laugh.

"Not funny," she groused. "It ain't just boys who are sensitive down there."

"I'm not surprised my house was trapped. Methuselah is very sly."

"Meth-who?" Hannah queried.

"The alien spirit that's causing all the curses. In a nutshell, a rock fell to Earth from space containing some kind of being who cast the fairytale curse. It's currently in a papier-mâché body, but it's looking to upgrade by taking over Killian's body."

To her credit, Hannah didn't burst out laughing at my outlandish recap. "Alrighty then. Magic-wielding body-snatching alien is our target. I knew this trip would be interesting. Where have they gone?"

I shrugged. "No idea and I doubt we'll figure it out before the body switch." Not with their head start.

"Giving up already?"

My lips turned down. "I don't want to, but we have no idea where they went."

"Yeah, we do." Hannah held up a phone. "Gerome's got a tracker in his spear. He had it installed when the airline folks lost it on a trip. He hunted it down and found it at a baggage unloader's home, but it took him a few days. We had the spear chipped after that."

"Assuming he has the spear with him," I pointed out.

"Gerome loves that sharp pointy stick more than anything. He'll have it," Hannah stated with confidence.

"Except Gerome isn't himself right now. Methuselah is controlling him."

"Just one more thing I can mock him with once we track them down. Let's go." Hannah waved us out.

We exited the room to see the house in shambles. Furniture broken and the broom that dared molest Hannah snapped in two.

Outdoors, the sun shone, bright and cheery. The day should have been heavy and dark like my heart. Poor Killian. I fretted about his wellbeing. Worried we wouldn't find him in time. Wondered when I'd fallen for the prince.

Hannah snapped her fingers. "Look sharp. We don't know what we'll encounter on our way back to the car."

"Can we even find it?" I asked as we followed Hannah out of the yard. "The mist—"

"Is gone." She pointed to the road we'd not seen when we'd arrived, dappled with sunlight.

"The rock, or should I say Methuselah, is constricted in how far and how much he can expend his power," Agatha declared. "The Grimm Effect curse is the only thing that doesn't seem to require much from him, and I can only assume it is a self-feeding spell."

"Why do you keep calling that alien jerk a he?"

"Because his arrogance and manners remind me very much of a man." Agatha sniffed.

Fair enough. Although I might stick to using "it." We followed the road, and as we walked, I asked Hannah what happened to her and Gerome.

"After that ash dragon spewed its cloud of fumes, Gerome went after it. No surprise there. Once it was gone, we realized we'd lost you and the prince, so we started looking, only a flock of geese came barreling through, hundreds of them, and we got separated. I tried looking for Gerome and even calling, but he didn't reply."

"Methuselah probably already had him bespelled by that point," Agatha's quiet addition.

"How come it never controlled you?" I asked, remembering how she'd claimed to have set it on fire.

"It tried." Agatha's look turned fierce. "But I'm a stubborn old lady. Guess it didn't stick. In good news, it doesn't last forever. From what I've observed with the townsfolk it used, the obeyance spell does eventually fade."

"So this alien, it's what? Trying to destroy the world by making us live out fairytales?" Hannah asked as we passed a pasture with some sheep. Sheep wearing remnants of clothes. Oh dear.

Agatha cleared her throat. "From what I've managed to glean, it thrives on chaotic emotion generated by the curses. So, for example, a Rapunzel, languishing for her prince, because the curse tells her she must have one, emits a force. That force feeds Methuselah, and as it grows, he can do things with it, like build forests overnight and transform people into beasts."

"Conjure mists and constructs," I muttered. "No wonder it called itself a god."

"More like a sorcerer, a bad one. And we all know what happens to bad magic-users," Hannah stated.

"They get houses dropped on them." I'd recently read the entire Oz collection.

Agatha chuckled. "I already know water doesn't work. I'd hoped he would be like those aliens in *War of the Worlds* when I dumped a bucket on it."

"Think more epic." Hannah spread her hands. "I'm talking like Voldemort and that dude from the *Lord of the Rings* movies."

"Um, they had wizards to fight them," I reminded. "We're not wizards.

"We'll find a way," Hannah assured.

I wished I had her confidence.

We encountered little resistance on our way to the car. Good sign or bad? Good in that we made good time, but bad because Methuselah obviously didn't think we posed a threat.

How long would it take to prep Killian and steal his body?

The car remained parked on the outskirts of the razed hamlet. We piled in, Godmother stuffing her skirts to fit in the back seat, while I took the passenger front.

Before driving, Hannah pulled out her phone and tapped the screen. "Let's see where my partner is," she muttered, loading an app. A map lit up her screen and displayed a blinking dot. She pointed to it. "They're moving fast."

"They're taking the A303," murmured Agatha.

"Any idea where they'd be heading? And why did Methuselah have to go elsewhere? Why not conduct the ritual at the cottage?" I had questions. Asking them helped me not languish in worry for Killian.

Agatha appeared pensive. "This is just a guess, but given their direction, and the fact Methuselah chose to relocate, I think they might be heading to Stonehenge."

"Why there?" I asked.

"Because it's an ancient mystical place of power." I glanced at Hannah in surprise, and she offered a defensive, "I like history, especially the stuff that might pertain to magic today."

"Stonehenge was abandoned centuries ago. I doubt it has any kind of magic left." Not to mention, I'd never heard of anything happening in or around it.

"Don't be so sure of that," Agatha piped in. "You know, I have to wonder if Methuselah spoke the truth about how the curse works."

"Why do you say that?"

"Because part of his explanation made no sense. How does deploying his magic create more magic?" Agatha exclaimed. "Expending magic should reduce, not increase, it."

"You're assuming magic follows scientific laws," I argued.

Agatha remained frowning. "Or Methuselah lied. He claimed to be weak when he arrived. Starving. And yet, within months, things began to happen."

"It called itself devourer of worlds. Most likely it began feeding upon arrival."

"Feeding on what, though?" Agatha kept thinking out loud. "He claimed the curses created the emotional turmoil that fed him energy, but why bother expending his limited resources casting his fairytale spell when so many people are already emotional messes?"

"If he's not eating their feelings, then it must be something else. Something it doesn't want us to know about," Hannah stated, her foot heavy on the pedal, making the poor little car put-put way faster than it was used to.

"Perhaps Methuselah can't touch the energy he craves directly. Could be he needs humans to channel it," I mused aloud.

"That would make sense, especially given he's not from Earth. You know, there's long been talk about ley lines running through the planet," Agatha commented. "Ley lines being energy conduits."

I snorted. "I know what ley lines are. Don't tell me you believe in them."

"I do, and if I'm right, it would make sense. You just said Methuselah might not be able to access magic without a conduit. AKA humans. If true, then perhaps he needs the curse to turn people into magnets for the Earth's natural power."

"If people became magic-magnets, then shouldn't they be the ones with the power?" I couldn't help my confusion.

"Unless the spell he casts draws in that energy but

then turns around and funnels it back to him," Agatha suggested.

"An interesting theory but let's say, even if it's true, how does that help? How are we supposed to cut him off?"

Agatha's lips turned down. "I don't know. But I do know he is very attached to his stone. I didn't realize until he locked me in that room that it was gone from the books. I can only assume he moved it."

"Or has it close by." I thought of the golem and how I thought I'd seen a spark of light when I sliced its chest. It led to me saying, "If we got hold of that stone and destroyed it—"

"That thing was living in outer space and crashed on Earth. You're not going to be able to smash it with a hammer." Hannah swerved around a slow-moving car, and I swear we lifted on two wheels as she passed.

"It might be indestructible. However, what about containment?" Agatha mused aloud. "If we could block the stone from emitting or receiving magic…"

"Then Methuselah would be powerless. But how are we supposed to A, get the rock from it, and B, contain it?"

Hannah ticked off possibilities. "Salt, salt water, lead, silver, iron."

"All human elements that might not work against an alien object," I pointed out.

"But might block the flow of Earthly magic," Hannah countered.

Might. Maybe. All of this spit-balling, while interesting, could be completely off base. What if there was no way of stopping Methuselah?

Then Killian would be screwed.

I had to find a solution before it was too late.

16

"The blinking dot stopped." I poked at the screen and zoomed in on the map. I craned to glance at Agatha lounging in the backseat. "You were right. They went to Stonehenge."

We had made good time following but were still about twenty minutes out, despite Hannah's insane racecar-driving tactics. Blame the time it took to walk to the hamlet where we'd parked.

"I don't think he'll have acted yet. The full moon isn't for a few hours," Agatha murmured.

"Does that make a difference?"

She shrugged. "Maybe? There are many who believe the full moon has power."

"People also used to think the Earth was flat and there were rain and crop gods." Despite this new world of magic and curses, I didn't believe all the folklore that had been passed down over generations.

"You know what's interesting?" Hannah suddenly spoke up. "We didn't have a single issue on the drive over."

I'd not even realized until she mentioned it.

"Because Methuselah thinks he's won," Agatha's low reply. "Why waste his energy when he's so close to getting what he wants?"

A reminder we had little time if we wanted to save Killian.

"Here's our exit," Hannah murmured as she guided us off the highway.

This late in the day, there wasn't any traffic on the road leading to the visitor center. Nor did we see any people. Just cows and sheep in the green grassy areas all around. Oddly, the parking lot held quite a few vehicles, including one that Agatha pointed to. "That's my car."

We parked and exited our ride for a glance around. Late afternoon would soon migrate to evening. I dreaded the moment I'd flip into fur. Especially since I now had the thought in my head that said each time I did, I might be feeding Methuselah.

"Where is everyone?" I murmured. The place appeared deserted. The visitor center, with its massive windows for walls, gave us a view of the inside. Tables, chairs, some knocked over. But no people. Odd for such a popular tourist spot, especially given all the cars and even buses parked nearby. Of more concern, the clothing strewn around. Shoes, pants, shirts, purses. My stomach tightened.

Hannah nudged me and pointed out to the grazing animals. "I do believe our alien wanted to ensure no one interfered."

It horrified me to realize he'd transformed them all. Innocent tourists with no idea a megalomaniac would ruin their day and life.

"Is it permanent?" I asked, horrified for them.

Agatha had a reply. "If they've been storyline cursed, then it will depend on the tale. If he just straight up changed them, then most likely it will wear off."

"Most likely isn't reassuring," I huffed.

"It's all I have, dear child. Until a few days ago, I'd never even spoken to Methuselah. All this information is new to me, and I have a feeling we've barely scratched the surface of what he can do."

More worrisome, he'd accomplished this as a paper puppet. How much worse would it be if he actually managed to get inside a human body? After all, if our theory was correct, and he needed humans to funnel Earth's magic, would possessing Killian's body give him direct access? I really didn't want to find out.

"We need to get to Killian." I began hiking in the direction of the stone monoliths, visible in the distance, casting shadows in the dipping sun.

"Hold on a second." Hannah grabbed me by the arm. "We need a plan."

I chewed my bottom lip. She had a point. However, my agitation didn't want to delay. "The plan is to get Killian and Gerome away from the golem."

"And then?" she prodded.

"I don't know. Shred the puppet?"

"You seem to have forgotten he doesn't need that simulacrum to act," Agatha reminded. "He spent decades like a spider in a web, pulling strings."

"Perhaps he doesn't need a body, but what about his rock?" The one that Agatha claimed Methuselah arrived in. The one he'd mentioned and hidden. "Maybe if we controlled it, we could control him?"

"Let's say we get it, then what? If smashing doesn't work, then what?" Hannah posed a serious question.

"There must be a way we can contain it so Methuselah can't act."

Hannah glanced towards the visitor center. "I wonder if they've got a gift box."

"Cardboard won't be enough." I ducked my head to think before exclaiming, "Maybe a bottle of water? Water tends to impede signals, doesn't it?"

"Water with some salt," Agatha suggested. "It's supposed to be good at containing spirits."

"I'll go check and see if they've got some kind of thermos for sale in their gift shop." Hannah's long stride took her to the only building in sight.

I slumped against the car and tried to not sigh.

"She is right. We can't rush in without a plan," Agatha said softly.

"I know. It's just the more time we waste, the less Killian has a chance to escape before that *thing* removes his soul and takes his body."

"You really care for him, don't you?"

"Yeah. More than expected," I admitted.

"I knew it," Agatha crowed. "And you thought I was crazy the night of the ball."

I glanced at her. "Wait, you knew that would happen?"

"Hoped. I've been observing people a long time. Couples especially, given my curse. You might say I've acquired a knack for putting the right people together."

My mouth rounded. "You cast a matchmaking spell?"

"Hardly. My magic isn't capable of that. More like I nudged you in each other's direction. And it worked even better than I could have imagined." She clasped her hands.

Imagined. The word rang in my head, nagging me. I found myself thinking. "You said the rock absorbed the stories from the books it came in contact with."

"Yes. I wish I'd set it upon my late husband's book on rocks. That might have saved us much grief. Why do you ask?"

"Are we sure the dark twist in them came from Methuselah?"

"Who else?"

"What if we, those cursed, are the ones warping it?" I thought of the nursery rhyme we'd brought to life, how the storm came when we concentrated on it hard enough. How we'd shaped our own magic.

"It's very possible. After all, if the curse has people absorbing magic to feed it, then I guess an individual could be using some of that power to influence the outcome and shape of their story."

"I might have a crazy idea." I dove into the car and began rummaging.

"What are you looking for?" Agatha asked.

"Something to write with." Nothing in the car. I eyed the visitor center. "I'll be right back."

I sprinted for the building and almost ran into Hannah coming out carrying a stainless-steel tumbler. "Found something," she chirped. "Filled with water and a shit-ton of salt."

"Perfect. Did you happen to see any stationary? Like a pen and paper?"

"I don't think a last will and testament is going to matter at this point," Hannah's dry response.

"It's for an idea I have. Might not work. Most likely crazy. But we've got nothing to lose." Except our entire world if it failed.

"Ooh, thinking outside the box. I like it. What's the plan? Going to write a letter to its mommy? Maybe a severely worded cease and desist?"

"I'm going to write its story."

Hannah blinked. "Er, come again?"

"The curse likes stories, right?" I didn't wait for her nod or reply. "It absorbs them and then tries to get them to replay, albeit with changes given our modern times. What if the curse absorbed the story of Methuselah's downfall?"

The suggestion pursed Hannah's lips. "You're right. It does sound crazy, but then again, this entire situation is bonkers."

"It can't hurt." I hoped. The way the curse twisted some stories might make this the worst idea ever. Or it might do nothing at all. After all, just writing the story wouldn't be enough, or every single book in the world would have been in play.

The gift shop had notepads and novelty pens. I perched on a table and began to scribble, writing as fast as I dared given the fact the sun kept sinking lower and lower meaning we ran out of time.

I couldn't get as detailed as I would have liked, but I managed to get something written that I hoped would work. I tucked the sheet in my pocket and hopped from the table. "Okay, I've got it."

"Wait, aren't you going to like read it aloud and activate it?"

I shook my head. "Not yet. This whole thing might hinge on us being close enough to Methuselah to act our parts."

"Parts? Wait, am I in this story?"

"We all are."

The story of a lifetime. I just hoped it wasn't our obituary.

17
Killian

CAPTURED AND WITHOUT A FIGHT.

Killian still couldn't believe how easily the monster behind the Grimm Effect managed to control him. Then again, what could he do when Gerome went after Belle and the thing in the papier-mâché body stated, "If you want her to live, then you'll do as I say."

In that moment, it didn't matter that the monster wanted to possess his body or that it had caused the world's woes. It threatened Belle's life, so Killian could only clench his fists and mutter, "Swear you'll leave her unharmed."

"Behave and she lives. Step out of line and there won't be enough left of her to recognize." A threat made all the worse for its flat delivery.

Did he trust the word of this alien? No. But a promise was better than nothing.

Gerome returned empty-handed and, even better, blood-free.

"The female?" the thing questioned.

"Is secured."

"Excellent. In that case, it is time for us to depart."

"Where are we going?" Killian asked.

"To a place where the magic is strong, strong enough for me to inhabit your shape and start the revolution of this world." The statement would have had a more chilling effect with an evil cackle. Instead, the paper puppet stiff-marched to the door.

Killian followed, although he did hesitate once he hit the sunshine. Was he really going to walk willingly to his demise?

He glanced back at the house. Gerome shoved him, and the thing reminded, "Obey or she perishes."

The threat led to him walking stiffly to the garage behind the cottage. He kept his gaze straight ahead, his shoulders back. Show no fear, a lesson instilled in him at a young age from his mother who said people would look for weakness that they could exploit. Confidence was the most important trait a ruler could have.

Even if faked.

The car ride proved uncomfortable, even though he had the entire back seat. He couldn't help but realize every mile they drove brought him closer and closer to the end.

Would removing his consciousness from his body hurt? Would he be a wraith, doomed to float the Earth? Would there even be an Earth left once Methuselah took over his life and began his plot for world domination?

It took just under two hours to reach their destination. The traffic on the highway moved rapidly, and they only stopped once for gas.

They pulled into the busy parking lot for Stonehenge, and Killian roused himself enough to ask, "Why are we here?"

"This is a place of power," Methuselah declared. "Not the strongest on your planet but enough to fuel my plans."

As they emerged, they got some strange looks. Blame the alien's appearance. In a world of fairytales that came to life, Methuselah still stood out. No one had ever seen the likes of him before. At the same time, people didn't point or comment. Just glanced, cocked their heads in puzzlement, and then went on with their day. In this case, being tourists.

Wait, make that sheep.

As they passed folks, some heading for their cars, others for the visitor center, waiting for their turn to see the wonder over yonder, sheep began to appear. It took Killian a second to realize what happened.

"What are you doing to those people?" he

exclaimed as an entire family turned into fuzzy-haired bleaters.

"Ensuring they don't interfere." The thing spoke matter-of-fact.

"By making them into sheep?"

"Isn't there an expression about sheep being good followers?" The thing didn't chuckle, and yet the mockery shone through loud and clear.

Moo. A few cows began popping up, and there was definite sarcasm as the puppet said, "There, some variety. Is that better?"

No. Nothing about this was good at all.

The distance from Belle finally gave him the push he needed to make a run for it. He bolted, heading back for the highway, where he could hitch a ride.

He didn't make it two paces before he froze in place.

"I wondered when you'd attempt to escape. You humans are so predictable," the thing chided. "Watch the prince while I handle the rest of the people."

The puppet master marched off, leaving in his wake more sheep.

Gerome stood by Killian's stiff and unmoving body, his arms crossed, his expression blank.

"Gerome, are you in there?" He tried appealing to the man.

No reply.

"You have to shake off whatever spell he's put you under. You're a Grimm Knight. You're supposed to be fighting this evil, not helping it."

Still not a single hint Gerome even listened.

"Think of Hannah."

Twitch. Just a single tic by Gerome's eye. Was she the key to freeing him?

"Hannah's going to be worried. I know you two are close."

Nothing.

No matter what Killian said, he didn't get another reaction. By the time the puppet returned, he was out of ideas.

"Time to handle those crowding the place of power. Follow." The command forced Killian's legs into motion. He walked like a tin soldier, left foot, right foot, following the paper butt to the crowd taking pictures of the stone structure.

He'd only ever seen pictures of Stonehenge. It loomed bigger than expected. Impressive, if you thought about it. The pillars with their crowning mantles erected in a time with no machines, just human hands and ingenuity.

People barely paid them any mind until Methuselah began forcing his way through the crowd.

"Hey, what the—*Baaa*." People began dropping to four hooves, which led to some panic. Screams began, as did a stampede to get away. None escaped the alien's curse, but the effort to change so many took its toll.

Killian noticed the puppet moving more sluggishly and stiff than before, as if weakened. Unfortunately, he couldn't say the same about the spell holding him, which seemed as strong as ever. He could observe. Blink. Nothing else.

"Let us see what we have to work with." Methuselah led the way into the stone circle, and Killian shivered as he passed the stones and didn't stop until he hit the dead center.

Was it him, or did the air hum? His hair certainly lifted, and his skin pimpled.

The simulacrum held out its arms and exclaimed, "Feel that power. Glorious, and soon it will be mine."

Killian would have loved to ask why it couldn't assess it now. Could that be the reason why it wanted his body?

The puppet pointed. "Lie down there."

Killian had no choice but to obey and lay on the grass, staring up at the blue sky. The sun was creeping for the horizon. Soon it would be night and Belle would transform alone for the first time.

How he missed her. A woman who'd stolen his interest with a vigorous tackle then taken his heart with her sass. He'd truly wanted to make their marriage work, knowing in her he'd found a partner for life.

Too fast? Not if you believed in love at first sight. He'd never been more sure than when she'd dropped that book and he knelt and gazed upon her, beautiful in her golden dress with her hair dressed in roses. In that moment, it hit him.

She's the one.

And now they'd never get a chance to explore what might have been.

"Stake him down. We don't want him moving around once I start." The simulacrum ordered Gerome, and the big man obeyed, leaving them only to return with metal pegs and rope, which he used to secure Killian to the ground.

The humbling nature of being unable to act didn't sit well. Killian usually liked to be in the thick of things. The one doing, not watching. Not this time. This time he got to be a spectator to his own demise.

Kind of depressing so he thought of happier things, like the carriage ride where he'd pleasured his wife. That had been one of the best moments of his life. He'd had plans to seduce her near a bed the next time to truly show her how she made him feel. Happy, energized, hopeful for the future.

Also scared, as he heard her voice suddenly. "That's enough. Leave him alone."

What was Belle doing here?

Being brave of course. He loved her for it but also wished she'd never come.

"Do not interfere," Methuselah stated, standing over him.

"I will so interfere," Belle huffed. "That's my husband."

Those words gave him the strength to turn his head to see her. She looked bedraggled and glorious with her hands planted on her hips. Still wearing the tracksuit she'd borrowed. Her hair a wild mess.

"Be still. The transference is about to begin," the puppet master stated as the sun set in a wild display of colors.

The last thing he would see apparently, as Methuselah crouched and whispered, "Time for you to vacate my new home."

And with that, his soul became untethered.

18

As we headed on foot for the stones, among which I could see a glimpse of that paper bastard, I lacked a full plan, but that didn't stop me. First things first.

"Hannah, you'll need to do something about Gerome." His dark-clad figure stood a few paces from my target.

"I ain't killing him," she stated flatly.

"No shit. I meant do something to distract so he doesn't interfere." Hopefully, handling Methuselah would snap him back to normal.

"Distract how?" Hannah asked.

"I don't know. Challenge him to a dance-off? A duel? Given how uptight he is, you might want to try a smooch."

Hannah recoiled. "Kiss him?"

"I know he's like a brother, but we're looking for shock value. Anything to keep him from helping the golem."

"And what will you be doing?" she queried.

"Trying to get close enough to Methuselah so I can grab his rock." Which I doubted would be easy.

"We don't know where the stone is," Godmother reminded softly, plodding along behind us.

"If it glows green, then I have a sneaking suspicion."

"You saw it?" Agatha exclaimed, verifying my theory.

"It's inside the puppet. I saw a green light when I stabbed him in the chest."

"How will you get it out?" Hannah asked as we got close enough to the stones to see clearly the two people standing within its ring and a third on the ground.

Please don't let me be too late.

My lips quirked. "It's almost sundown, and this time I'm eager to welcome the beast." Especially its shredding claws.

Hannah slapped me on the back. "Good luck."

"What am I to do?" Agatha asked.

"Hold on to this, and if you spot a chance to give it to the rock, take it." I handed her my quickly scribbled story.

Agatha clutched it tight and nodded. "Luck be with you, dear child."

I'd need more than luck to make this work.

Despite not hiding our approach, neither Methuselah nor Gerome turned around to watch our arrival. As if we didn't matter. Kind of insulting but, then again, let them think we didn't pose a threat. I'd take any advantage I could get.

I stepped within the stone ring, and my heart stopped at the sight of Killian staked to the ground and the golem looming over him.

Despite my racing heart and sweaty palms, my voice sounded steady and strong when I shouted, "That's enough. Leave him alone."

"Do not interfere," Methuselah stated without turning its head.

"I will so interfere," I huffed. "That's my husband."

Mine. And I'd not yet gotten a proper wedding night, just a tantalizing precursor.

Killian struggled to turn his head, and when he did, his brilliant gaze met mine. I could see the fear in his eyes, fear for me, not himself, my foolish brave prince.

As the sun began to set, Methuselah uttered a sharp command. "Keep her away. The transference is about to begin."

Time enough to disrupt whatever convoluted ritual Methuselah would perform.

Gerome planted himself in my path, not that I let that stop me from racing in his direction while Hannah came at him from the side. *Please don't let him hurt her*. I'd feel bad. He'd feel bad. But we had no choice. To free him from Methuselah's mind control, we had to take out the one causing the problem.

Since Gerome remained fixated on me, he didn't do a thing to stop Hannah when she dove and took him out at the knees. She knocked him down, and I leaped past their tussling bodies, only to have my rush abruptly halted with one word from the golem.

"Stop."

Poised on one leg, my hands still reaching, frozen in place.

"I'll deal with you once I'm done," the alien promised.

It stood by Killian's head, and I expected chanting, at the very least some handwaving. None of that happened. The paper puppet neither moved nor spoke, yet a spark emerged from Killian's body, a glowing speck—his soul! My prince's eyes went blank.

I was too late.

No! I screamed in silence since Methuselah had stolen my voice. Stolen my ability to move. Stolen everything from me, including the man I'd fallen for.

The alien placed its hands on its paper chest, and it burned, the hardened surface turning black and flaking away until a gaping hole appeared. Within that cavity floated a sphere glowing a bright green. It emerged, floating midair just as the sun set and my curse activated.

The beast burst free from my body, and this time, I embraced it. Even better, not only did it rip my humanity away in that moment but it shredded the compulsion keeping me frozen.

"Get away from him," I growled once the transformation finished.

Methuselah didn't turn his head but did utter a command. "I told you to not let her interfere."

I couldn't help a low chuckle. "Gerome is busy."

Indeed, Hannah had lured him from the alien's side. Gerome had his spear in hand but appeared to be hesitating to strike the dancing Hannah who taunted him.

"Guess it's just you and me." I grinned. Probably with a lot of teeth.

Not that Methuselah cared or showed any reaction. He grabbed hold of the bright rock and bent with it.

My horrified eyes saw a small slice appear on Killian's chest, fabric and skin parting despite there being no knife. Blood welled, and I knew if the rock got within that flesh it was all over. I roared and charged, slamming into the puppet before it could insert the stone.

It didn't grunt or react in pain. Not even when I shredded its paper body with my claws. I tore off its arms, slivered its torso, ribboned its head until it collapsed inward.

I knelt, huffing over the inert carcass. Had I done it? Agatha didn't think I could kill it so easily. She was most likely right, but by taking away its golem I'd slowed it down at least, which meant time to locate the stone.

A glance to my left showed it glowing in the grass. I scrabbled for it, only to freeze as a chunky sheep bounded over and lapped it up with a fat tongue. The glow disappeared in its mouth, but more disturbing, it spoke. "You can't win."

More sheep approached, each speaking with his voice.

"I am mightier than you."

"I am stronger."

"Wilier."

"You're delicious as a chop," I growled as I swiped for the one that had gobbled the rock.

It spat it out as I went to grab it by the scruff and impaled itself on my claws. It hit the ground, legs twitching, and to my horror, the fuzzy body turned back into a human.

A dead person. Shit.

While I stared in shock, another sheep picked up the stone.

"Give me that," I huffed, only to see the sheep huddling close and shuffling, a shell game of moving animals, making me lose track of which one had it.

"Argh," I railed.

Cackling erupted from all the remaining sheep. "Will you kill them all?"

"If that's what it takes to stop you." I'd deal with the guilt later.

"Kill them. It doesn't matter. I'll use your body, if I must, to complete the transference."

"You wouldn't like my body. I've got this troublesome mole that needs removing, and my joints on rainy days... I wouldn't wish those on anyone," I babbled.

"I won't be requiring it for long," spoke the one facing me. "Once the stone is embedded into the empty container, I shall enjoy using his hands to kill you."

Good to know it needed embedding for full takeover and not just a simple touch. Now to make sure it didn't happen, but for that, I needed to locate the sheep that had the rock.

I might have never figured it out but for the fact I

noticed one of the furry critters heading for Killian. I lunged and tackled the beast, making it squeal loud enough to hurt my ears. This time, I didn't kill it. I did, however, lift it up in the air by its hind legs and give it a vigorous shake, and then I kept shaking it until something bright and green flew out of its mouth.

"You are annoying me!" screeched the angry alien, and I had to admit being impressed it could force a sheep to speak. Oddly, it hadn't done anything worse. No dragons or flocks of birds. Could it be Methuselah had been using too much magic? It might explain why it couldn't subdue me. I couldn't waste this advantage.

I dropped the ewe and went after the green glow. I'd bent to grab it when the ground rippled, sending it tumbling. Then it was floating...

Toward Killian!

No. And no.

I raced to block it, managing to dive and slap it away from my husband. It sailed away between the stones, and the sheep all screamed in frustration.

Finally, the alien showed some emotion.

I loved it.

Gerome appeared behind a sheep, glaring at me balefully. Guess I knew which body the alien currently controlled. The sheep suddenly contorted, losing its wool, until an old man, partially hunched, stood there naked.

"You are annoying me," the man declared before pointing a gnarled finger. "About time you took care of that Knight. Get rid of the woman and then find my rock."

"Fuck you," Gerome grunted.

Yesss!!! The grumpy Knight was back in action. A bemused-looking Hannah, her cheeks flushed and eyes bright, joined him.

"Shall we dance?" she asked Methuselah in his borrowed body.

"No," a flat reply before the man collapsed.

Before I could ask where Methuselah struck next, Hannah clutched her head. "Oh no you don't," she growled.

The alien spirit was trying to possess her. Gerome glanced at me. "Get the rock. I've got her."

To my surprise, the big Knight wrapped his arms around her, but not to crush. He lifted her for a kiss.

She relaxed in his grip, and the whispering started in my head.

Let me in.

Oh hell no.

You can't win. I am stronger than you. Stronger than all of you.

"Says the alien with no body. No army. Nothing." I spoke aloud and was rewarded with a piercing shriek that made me wince.

Then nothing. I whirled around, looking to see who he'd taken over. The old man huddled on the ground, sobbing. Killian remained still. Hannah was kissing Gerome, and well, let's just say they might want to get a room given where his hands were roaming.

Where had Methuselah gone?

The sheep huddled in a group, close enough it seemed as if they were overlapping.

Hold on. They were. The sheep were merging, fusing together, their muzzles open wide as they *baa*-ed in terror.

"What the hell?" I blinked, and yet that didn't change the fact a mega-monster-sheep took form. Its body a giant wooly barrel. The heads had combined to form a huge noggin that grew teeth and horns. Its stubby yet thick legs ended in hooves.

It stamped a foot and lowered its crown of tines before charging.

At me.

Guess I'd pissed it off.

Gerome uttered a cry and ran at it with his spear, launching it. The pointed end entered the flank of the monster, and it roared, its voice a raspy rumble. "Your puny stick can't kill me."

Its mouth opened wide, and I saw a glow forming in its throat.

Was it going to spew fire like a dragon?

As it blew, I dove to the side, hitting the ground hard.

Sssss.

The sizzling sound had me glancing to the spot where I'd been standing, slimed and smoldering.

"It's spitting acid!" I yelled.

Which might be worse than fire, judging by how it burned the ground.

The monster trotted for me, readying another blast, when Agatha suddenly appeared, holding the green stone aloft. "I wouldn't do that if I were you."

The mega-sheep-monster paused.

"It's past time we put a stop to your terrorizing," Agatha huffed. She pulled the canister of salt water from a pocket in her skirt. She grumbled a bit as she struggled to unscrew the cap. She plopped the rock inside.

The mega-sheep chuckled. "Oooh. I'm terrified. Water can't harm me," it mocked.

"This is magical water," Agatha declared. "And this is a special chalice made to hold aliens with nefarious intent."

"There is no such th—"

She screwed the lid shut before it finished its sentence, and suddenly, the mega sheep monster collapsed. And by collapsed, I mean the bodies of the humans used to make it tumbled apart to land in a bloody pile that turned my stomach.

Agatha beamed. "We did it."

The bottle shook.

"It's fighting," I murmured.

"I don't think it's going to hold," Hannah hollered.

"It will if we use magic. Agatha, where's the story?" I replied.

"Here. I read it to the bottle a few times to get it ready." She handed me the slip of paper, and I started to read what started out as a story but turned into a bad limerick.

There once was an asshole from space,
   who came to rock our Earthly base.
   It inhabited a book,
   the stories overtook,
   and turned our world into a fairytale place.

The people of Earth suffered,
   we had no magic of our own to buffer.
   Until along came an unlikely group,
   who set out on a quest to recoup
   and vanquish the alien invader.

. . .

The heroes found themselves in England,
 a prince, his wife, and their liegemen.
 For the final battle they braced,
 in a very old and magical place,
 where our heroes took their last stand.

Luckily, they had a special chalice,
 the type that could hold malice.
 They filled it with holy water
 in hopes it would hold the squatter
 and end a curse most callous.

The alien's influence was shattered.
 No one could hear its chatter.
 Sealed in its tomb,
 it was very doomed,
 with no way to bloom,
 And the world lived happily ever after.

Hannah snorted. "You wrote a fucking poem?"

"Actually, it's a bad limerick," I grumbled.

"I don't think it worked." Agatha struggled to hold on to the agitated thermos.

"Let me try again." I recited the poem, to no effect, but Hannah neared me. "Maybe it needs all of us again, like with the storm we called."

"There is power in belief and numbers," Agatha agreed as they crowded close and we recited my terrible limerick as the full moon rose and bathed us in its light.

We chanted it over and over until Agatha whispered, "Something's happening."

The bottle stopped trembling.

And so we said it again, with gusto, singing it, shouting it, putting our everything into those verses until...

Poof.

We suddenly had an enclosed chalice of swirling gold and silver, intricately carved, sealed shut, and, best of all, still and silent.

We'd done it.

We'd imprisoned Methuselah.

19

With Methuselah secured, for the moment at least, I rushed to Killian's side, falling to my knees by his prone body. His chest rose and fell, and he remained warm to the touch.

"Wake up," I huffed, shaking him to no avail. His flesh might live, but his soul, the spark that animated Killian, remained absent. "No," I murmured. I couldn't believe I'd failed. I'd had one focus coming to Stonehenge. One mission—save my prince—and instead he was in a coma that he'd never wake from.

Devastated, my tears fell upon his face, and I hugged him to my chest, rocking and sobbing. What use was a victory against the alien invader when I couldn't save my prince?

"I'm so sorry," I whispered through a throat tight

with grief. Sorry for what could have been. Sorry we'd not had more time.

I sniffled against him and wished I'd done more.

Wished I'd said three words—I love you.

WELL, this was quite the dilemma. While Methuselah didn't kill Killian, he did worse. He untethered Killian's soul from his body, leaving him afloat and discombobulated.

An odd sensation and annoying state of being. For one, Killian found it hard to stay in one place. Every hint of a breeze pushed his ghostly aura away from the spot holding his body, whereas propelling his soul proved challenging. No feet or legs nor hands... How was he supposed to get around? Ghosts made it look easy, simply floating where they wanted.

Not Killian. He drifted away from his body, bumping into the stone arches, which, surprisingly, proved to be solid enough to keep him from leaving the area entirely. It left him a spectator to the action, although that might be a misnomer. He didn't see as he used to, rather everything had an aura. The ground a pale brown. The sky and air around a very light blue. People shone the brightest. He guessed by what he'd last seen that the bright silver people-shapes belonged to Gerome and Hannah, whereas Belle exuded a gorgeous gold. It shouldn't surprise Methuselah emitted a sickly green.

Identifying which colors belonged to whom meant Killian could track the spirit of the alien even when it temporarily merged with dull orange spots that, at one point, joined together to form an orange mega-blob.

It annoyed that the alien spirit so easily jumped in and out of bodies, while Killian, with a perfectly fine shape on the ground, the gold of it fading the longer he was absent, couldn't seem to climb back into his.

While his vision might not work the same, Killian could hear. Hear as his friends and wife fought the alien-created monster. Heard when they outsmarted Methuselah and, even better, saw when the alien's sickly glow suddenly disappeared. They'd done it. They'd won!

Only it wasn't a true victory.

Belle sobbed over Killian's fading body. He wished he could comfort her. Wished they'd had more time. He managed to push himself from the stone arch and drifted in her direction, drawn by her grief. He managed to hover above her glow, and while he couldn't touch her, he merged his aura with hers, trying to show her comfort.

This wasn't fair. His body was right there. Surely, there was a way back to it.

Despite her not speaking aloud, he heard her say, *I love you.*

He only wished he could tell her he loved her too.

Uh-oh.

A sudden suction had a hold of his spirit, and there was no fighting it.

Nor did he want to when he realized it sucked him back into his body.

It took a disorienting second before he could blink his eyes, and it took a moment more before he managed to rasp out, "Don't cry, wifey poo. You're getting your fur wet."

"Killian?" She shrieked his name and then almost broke him with a beast-strength hug. "I thought you were gone."

He sat up and dragged her into his lap, murmuring, "Me too."

"We beat Methuselah," she crowed.

"I know. Very clever feeding the stone a story meant to trap it."

She leaned her head against him. "I didn't think it would work."

"But it did. You saved the world. Saved me," he murmured.

"I hope so," she huffed. "Although looks like it didn't remove the curse. I'm still a beast."

"Your fur is soft," was his reply.

She snorted. "Not helping."

Agatha joined them, eyes bright. "What a glorious day for everyone."

"Only one thing could make this better," Killian quipped.

To which everyone replied, "Food!"

Only it didn't happen quite that quickly. First, Belle and the Knights had to make some calls to inform the Fairytale Bureau of what had transpired. That led to unmarked cars and vans arriving, spilling out agents, all of whom had questions.

The chalice holding Methuselah was regarded with caution and was taken away by a pair of people in hazmat suits, with it nestled inside a locked lead-lined case. Statements were taken, but when they would have transported them all to the nearest bureau for in-depth questioning, Killian put down his foot.

"It's been a long day, and my wife and I are exhausted. You've got enough to work with for now."

The prince had spoken, and rather than cause a diplomatic incident, appointments were scheduled for them to come in and make proper depositions, as well as answer any new questions that arose.

The group was allowed to leave, the five of them crammed in the tiny car, which puttered them to the nearest hotel, where his name alone secured them three rooms for the night.

As he and Belle entered their suite, she ducked her head. "I'll sleep on the floor."

"Why?"

"Because no one wants to sleep with an oversized furball."

"I do." He held out his hand. "Snuggle me. I've had a rough day."

And thus did they spoon, not saying much, just holding each other as exhaustion took them.

Dawn was only hours away, and he wanted a bit of sleep before he finally and properly seduced his wife.

20

Despite my exhaustion, I woke in the wee hours before dawn to a gun in my face. In the defense of the person holding it, I was still a monster. Not that the woman with steely hair and even steelier eyes cared, as she glared at me and snapped, "What have you done with my son?"

The queen looked as if she'd shoot me if I didn't give the right answer. I didn't need to glance to know Killian was no longer in bed, and we didn't have the Knights watching us because, as Killian told them the night before, "I want alone time with my wife."

When Hannah argued, "We're supposed to guard you," he countered with, "Against what? Methuselah has been imprisoned. I no longer have women tossing shoes at my head since I got married, and I've got the toughest beast around to handle anything that might happen." To appease, though, he got them the room directly across the hall.

A single room with a single bed because Gerome had grunted at check-in, "No need for two."

And to my shock, Hannah blushed.

The queen glared at me, and I murmured, "I don't know where he is."

Wrong answer. The gun cocked, and I really thought she'd shoot me in the face before Killian snapped, "Get that gun out of my wife's face, Mother." Killian emerged from the hotel bathroom with lips downturned.

The woman glanced between him and me before uttering an incredulous, "You married a beast?"

"Bah, more like a cuddly kitten," he stated, crawling onto the bed and sitting beside me.

"You can't be serious," his mother exclaimed. "You're my heir. What will people think if they know you're married to one of the monsters?"

"I don't care what anyone says or thinks. I love her, and that's all there is to it."

He loved me?

I wasn't the only one surprised by his admission. "If you love her so much, then prove it. Kiss the beast." His mother waved the gun.

I protested. "No. Don't make him do that. It's gross." I wouldn't want to kiss myself, not in this shape.

But Killian wasn't me, and he never backed down from a dare.

"If you insist." He leaned in and pressed his mouth to mine. His human lips to my furry-ringed beast ones.

He kissed me as if I weren't a monster.

Kissed me because he loved me.

And it hurt!

My body crackled and shrank. I gasped. Not because of the pain but the time. It wasn't yet dawn, and yet the beast body was gone. "I'm cured!"

Kilian looked smug as he said, "Guess my kisses are magic."

"It's called true love's kiss," his mother declared, tucking away her gun. "It can cure just about anything."

So it appeared and I had to wonder now about those beasts who kept claiming they needed sex with a willing virgin. Could it be the curse never needed the innocence of a hymen but rather love, freely given? A love that didn't care about appearance. Love that valued a person for who they were and not the shell containing it. It made sense. After all, Blanche and Cinder had been cured of their curses when they found true love.

Killian gave me a quirky smile. "Wish we'd thought to do that last night." He winked, and I blushed because I understood what he meant.

His mother, however, pretended to be oblivious. "I hear you were on an—"

Slam. The door got kicked open, and Gerome, wearing only briefs, and Hannah, in his shirt, popped in, gun and spear out, ready to fight.

Killian shouted, "It's just my mom. No threat."

"You must be the Knights who helped my son," the queen stated.

"Just doing our job," Hannah replied with a shrug.

"You went above and beyond with your bravery." The queen beamed. "You both have to come to Corsica that I might honor you for your actions."

"Do we have to?" Gerome whispered to Hannah.

She nudged him and stated, "Perhaps if our schedule permits." She then glanced at me. "No fur."

"Killian fixed me."

Hannah arched a brow, and I blushed as I stammered, "No, we did not do that. It only took a kiss of true love to break the curse."

"Oh." Hannah blushed again, and I wondered why until I remembered how she'd distracted Gerome who currently only wore underpants.

The queen clapped her hands. "I don't know

about you, but I'm hungry. Shall we adjourn to the dining establishment and discuss events?"

"You go ahead, Mother. I'll be along in a few minutes after I shower."

Killian turning down food? I almost asked if he was okay. His mother frowned, but before she could open her mouth, Hannah had a hold of her arm and murmured, "If Your Majesty will give me a moment to dress, I'll escort you downstairs."

"Like I need any help. I can defend myself," the indignant queen huffed.

She left with the Knights, the door not quite shutting behind them.

Killian shook his head. "Not how I'd planned for you to wake up," he stated, wedging a chair under the knob since the splintered frame wouldn't let the door latch.

"And how exactly did you plan to rouse me?"

He turned a devilish grin on me. "How about I show you?"

It started with a kiss and some groping. The clothes went next. The skin-to-skin contact proved electric to someone who'd never experienced that sensation.

He murmured, "I'd like to take my time exploring every inch of you—"

"But your mother is liable to come kicking down the door if we take too long," I finished. I also laughed. "To be honest, I don't think I can stand to wait another second." Brazen words.

"Me either." He chuckled. "It's been hell keeping my hands off you since the wedding."

"Really?"

"Yes, really. You are amazing, Annabelle. I'm so glad you're my wife. I love you, and I promise, while your first time might be a little uncomfortable, it's normal and—"

I hushed him. "I'm a virgin and not." Then before he could ask, "I've been using toys for years. At first, I thought it might get rid of the beasts, but losing my hymen didn't stop them. I kept using them after because I assumed those would be my only lovers in this lifetime. I hope you're not disappointed."

"More like relieved. I never want to cause you pain. Only pleasure."

With that, he kissed me and touched me. But when he would have gone down on me, I murmured, "I want to come with you inside me." Wanted to know how it felt.

And so he filled me. Filled me with his manhood, and it stretched me delightfully. It felt better than a toy. With him, I experienced nirvana.

Even better, as we showered off in a rush to make it to breakfast before his mom came storming back, he made me a promise.

I will cherish you forever, for you are the one I've been waiting for. The love of my life.

Epilogue

While the evil spirit controlling the Grimm Effect remained bound—not just in the magical chalice but also wrapped in iron, then a layer of silver, then lead, before being buried in hallowed ground under a temple the Grimm Knights guarded twenty-four-seven—the curse remained active in our world. Those already affected kept playing out their story, but at least with some, we knew what would cure it. True love.

An unexpected side effect? Excess magic. With Methuselah no longer siphoning the power from humanity affected by the curse, people began to wield this new power. Some could do wondrous things—healing being the most positive aspect. Others could be quite terrifying like those who used it to raise the dead.

It also affected the world at large, transforming it.

For example, unicorns appeared, galloping down streets or through yards, pristine white, with glowing manes and glowing horns. Then there were the darker versions, named the night furies, with red eyes, fur dark as night, their hooves striking sparks as they gored those in their path with their obsidian horns.

Mermaids began to crop up in oceans around the world.

Dragons multiplied, fighting over territory and stealing sheep.

The mountains became the property of dwarves.

Elves ruled the forests.

It meant the Knights and the bureau were busier than ever.

As for me? I was a princess in Corsica, but before you think I was involved in all that political mumbo-jumbo, I had a different job. Since the island only ever had transient agents, I opened an official Fairytale office, and to my delight, my friends chose to be the agents working it, because, as Cinder declared, "If I'm going to work, why not in paradise?"

Hood also joined me with her wolfish husband. In his case, true love didn't make him fully man again. But me? I was beast-free and in love.

Life was better than any story in a book. Even with my overbearing mother-in-law. But I kind of enjoyed the coddling I'd never gotten as a child, especially when I got big with twins.

My husband doted on me, and when those babes were born, I'd never seen him look so happy—unless sexy times counted.

And when little Morgana began throwing lightning bolts from the crib and Arthur changed into a little furry beast each time he had a tantrum, my husband took it in stride. Rubber room for the wee princess to avoid fires. Jungle gym for the energetic prince.

Every day was a new story in our fairytale, and I, for one, wouldn't change a thing about my happily ever after.

HOPE YOU ENJOYED *this series inspired by some amazing covers. I love it when I can see an image and a story smacks me. While you might be sad this storyline is done, do check out my website (EveLanglais.com) for something to tempt you.*

www.ingramcontent.com/pod-product-compliance
Lightning Source LLC
LaVergne TN
LVHW031539060526
838200LV00056B/4577